Shug's Daddy

SIOBHAN SMILE

Hostile
WHISPERS PRESS

SHUG'S DADDY

SIOBHAN SMILE

HOSTILE WHISPERS PRESS

SHUG'S DADDY

Grey

I was just a divorced, small-town, hardware store owner, and the man most people considered a gentleman. A slip up in my strict routine would send the town gossips into a frenzy. Yet I'd grown up in that town and everyone knew everyone. No secrets were safe, but I carried one that would send my world into chaos if I let it. I was falling for a town transplant and one of my best friends, Sugar. He was everything I wasn't. Spontaneous, fun, and knew exactly who he was. What would he see in a boring man like me?

Sugar (Shug)

I was that fat, femme, gender nonconforming person who hadn't known the inside of a closet in my life. With a mom like mine, she taught me to never live with regrets, but I had a massive one. I fell in love with my straight, gentlemanly best friend. Grey was everything I wasn't. Thankfully, he was clueless, but our shared friend group wasn't. How long could our friends stay silent in a town as small as ours?

1

GREY

THE OLD BELL CHIMED OVER THE DOOR OF MY HARDWARE store as I poured myself my fourth coffee of the day. My place was open from six AM to six PM, six days a week, and closed on Sundays. Same as when my old man ran the place, unlike with him, though, I had a few employees who gave me time off when I needed it. Yet, I only used them in cases of emergencies. I'd never been a man who asked for help. I darted a glance at my first customer, Sugar Mitchell. His high heels clicked on the battered hardwood floors.

The younger man always put me on edge, and I could never figure out why. He was a beautiful, softly built man. He carried himself with exuberance and pride. Shug, as everyone called him, was the exact opposite of me in all ways. I was jealous of the openness he had with anyone and everyone. Having a conversation with me was like pulling teeth. Most people gave up after I wouldn't engage with more than mono-syllables, but Shug never did.

Jenkins, Montana, for a small town, had a large LGBTQ population and had always had couples and people who lived openly. My dad had said when people grew up, they loved differently and there wasn't anything wrong with it. As long as two consenting adults were happy, who were we to judge? Dad had been vocal about discrimination when he saw someone who thought they were better than anyone else. It didn't matter if it was race or sexuality, gender. To my parents, everyone was equal, and I'd learned that early.

"Good morning, Grey." His glossy lips tugged into a smile. His five o'clock shadow was more for fashion than not shaving in the morning.

"Morning. How can I help you?" I'd tentatively called us friends; we shared the random lunch a few times a week and met up on the rare outing friends forced me to attend.

"My house was an icebox when I got up. My nipples could cut glass and not for any fun reasons." He batted his long, thick lashes at me, and for the hundredth time, I wondered if they were fake.

I shook my head, and he winked at me. "Give me your key."

He immediately shook his head. "You don't have to do it yourself. I'm sure you have better things to do."

"Shug, give me your key. I might not get to check at lunch, but I'll be by after I get off. I pass by your place on my way home. You work until six, right?" He owned a plus-sized boutique on Main Street and did a good online business. I loved listening to him talk about his shop. He became animated when he talked; he'd lean in with such a bright smile you couldn't help but return it.

"Yes, sir. I close at six, but normally don't finish paperwork and online orders until sometimes seven," he said as he worked a key off the ring.

"If you're not home by the time I'm finished, I'll wait." I picked up the key he laid on the counter, removed my keyring, and slipped it on beside mine so I wouldn't lose it.

"You don't have to do that, just leave—"

"Shug, I'll wait." While our small town was progressive in

most ways, there were still bigots around, I wouldn't leave his key for anyone with the initiative to look to pick it up.

"Okay, thank you. I'm going to have breakfast at the diner. Would you like me to bring you something?"

"No, thank you. I had breakfast before I left home."

"Of course, you did. You probably even pack your lunch and cook dinner every night."

"Yes, I do." Did he think I was boring like everyone else? I didn't drink or rarely went to the local bars. I preferred being home. Taking a ride on one of my horses around my property before I settled in for the night with a movie or a book. I wasn't exciting, but my life was calm and the way I wanted it.

"So nice and responsible, all adult."

"Nothing wrong with that." Without thinking, I defended my life choices. I knew people thought I was too stoic and reserved. I'd married my high school sweetheart after college, and we'd spent ten years together before she found my life too simple and routine. She'd left for excitement. I'd been a confirmed and abstinent bachelor since then, even though ladies in town tried to flirt, but it always made me feel awkward.

"No, sir, there isn't. Could I make you dinner for helping me?"

"That's unnecessary. If I can't fix it myself, you'll have to pay someone. I'll build fires for you so you stay warm."

"It was one time, Grey, one." He held up his index finger with a long, manicured painted nail. Today was dark purple with some flower design.

My lips twitched as I remembered the gossip of Shug trying to build his first fire when he moved to town and smoked up his entire house when he hadn't opened the flue. The fire department had found him on his lawn in a pink robe having a meltdown that he'd burned down his house.

"It wasn't funny. Hot firefighters and I wasn't looking my best. I was a mess, honey, a mess."

"I heard you made quite the first impression."

"You're an evil man, and I no longer like you."

He spun and stomped from the store. I kept it together until the door slammed behind him, and he glared at me through the age-etched glass. I lifted my mug to my mouth to cover my smile as he walked away adorably huffy.

I had to admit his presence had made the last five years interesting. A visit from him wasn't boring and broke up my normal routine. The bell going off again reminded me I needed to focus on work.

THAT NIGHT AT A QUARTER AFTER SIX, I'D OPENED THE front door of Shug's small single-story house. The interior made me smile at the colorful explosion of furnishing and curtains, rich fabrics, and a few creepy mannequins dressed in wild outfits of feathers and sequins and massive headpieces. One of them reminded me of his Halloween costume the prior year. From what I could picture from that night, it left little to the imagination. He'd been on his way to a costume party at one of the local bars as I left work. He'd flashed me with a wink, and he'd had yellow lashes that had to be at least three inches in length.

Before checking his furnace, I made sure the fireplaces in his living room and bedroom were safe. Unlike the rest of his house, I hadn't looked around his personal space. I'd brought over enough wood to last a few days in case I couldn't fix whatever was wrong with his heating. The house was old and in need of work. The elderly lady who'd owned it before hadn't kept up the maintenance the last few years of her life. She was a hermit, the one who elicited rumors, but every small town had at least one. Shug was just trying to make the Band-Aids last longer. His time may be up, though.

I grabbed my toolbox I'd left beside the door and made my

way to the basement. I wasn't overly tall, but I had to bend almost in half to make my way across the musty space. I pulled the chain on the bare bulb in the center of the room. It didn't help much, but thankfully Shug didn't use the basement for storage.

A quick glance at my watch told me I'd had about thirty minutes before I should expect Shug home. I got to work. The house wasn't cold to me, but I knew he'd moved there from California, and every fall and winter, Shug dressed like he was getting ready to trek across Antarctica.

As time passed, my curses became worse as I diagnosed the furnace dead on arrival. Nothing seemed wrong with the breakers, and the water heater was working fine. A closing door and the click of heels echoed above my head, and I cleaned up my tools to make my way upstairs.

"Hey, do I have heat?"

He peeked out of the kitchen, and his usually artfully styled black hair was falling over his forehead. I'd never seen him less than perfect before. He was no less pretty for a man. The first time I met him, I asked what his pronouns were, and he'd acted shocked. Maybe he hadn't expected a small town to be somewhat enlightened.

"Unfortunately, no, the lady who owned the place before didn't keep everything in working order. You're going to need a new furnace. I'll call someone I know when I get home to come out tomorrow. I brought a few days' worth of wood to keep you warm, but if it's longer than that, I'll drop off more."

"How much do I owe for you coming out and for the firewood?"

"Nothing, if I needed a part, I would've just charged you for that."

The need to argue tensed his body. I loved his independence. Yet, I also knew allowing himself to accept help wasn't easy for him. He knew better than to argue with me, though, so with an eye roll, he relaxed.

"Can I make you a cup of coffee?"

"That would be nice. I'm going to take my tools outside and then get to work on your fires. You should watch so you know the proper way to start one."

"I know how to start one. I just forgot to open the flue, and then the panic set in."

"Okay."

"I don't like that you're placating me."

"Yes, dear."

"If I wasn't more polite, I'd flip you off right now."

A loud grumpy sigh followed me out of the house, and I got started on carrying in the firewood. Dividing it between the two stone fireplaces. I started the first one in his bedroom, and once I was sure it would stay going, I headed for the living room and peeked into the kitchen to find him watching the coffee pot.

"Just need to take care of the living room, and then I can get out of your way."

He turned with a smile. "You're fine. It's nice to come home to someone. My life before I moved here was chaotic. Even five years later, the quiet sometimes gets weird."

"I never asked, why did you move here? Not a booming metropolis."

I'd known the former owner of the boutique, Deena. She'd talked about moving away for years to be near her son and maybe enjoy some warmth and downtime. Everyone was a little shocked when she'd announced she'd sold her place to a guy from California. It was the popular gossip for nearly six months before Shug showed up in town with a moving trailer.

"I think that's why. Deena and I met; her son hung around my group of friends. She came for a visit, and we hit it off. We started corresponding online, keeping up with each other, and she knew I wanted to own a shop one day. I think, in some ways, she became a mentor of sorts. She offered me first option to buy it. After some thought and looking over the mail-order options for sustainability, I decided why not, right?"

Even though I meant to go home, I took the mug of coffee he offered and stepped deeper into the kitchen. The same colorful chaos extended to every room.

"Must have been a culture shock."

"Not really, my mother is very...spiritual and nomadic. I spent a lot of time in ashrams and communes in remote places. No, I got the full culture shock experience when I moved to California. I was sixteen, and I barely knew how to tell time."

"What?"

"I only knew time in relation to seasons, or yesterday and today. Mom taught me that yesterday already happened. It was no more important than the lessons it taught you. Tomorrow doesn't exist, so we shouldn't worry about a time that hasn't occurred yet. Today..." He took a sip of his coffee. "Today mattered, what you learned, how you affected change and positivity on others who may not have had as much love as you. We live in the now because a minute, an hour or a day, well, there's no guarantee."

"Refreshing but not always sustainable." I couldn't imagine living in the moment. To not plan or worry about what the next day brought was a nightmare for me.

He leaned back against the counter and raised his mug to his mouth. A serene expression on his face. I think that's why I always felt at ease but also on edge around him. He was so comfortable in who he was and didn't let the environment around him get him down. I was always the shy loner who preferred my quiet over the chaos. He'd be able to fit in anywhere.

"No, it wasn't, especially when you're a sixteen-year-old who made all your own clothes and never experienced bullying. Was out since you were running around in rainbow cloth diapers. Or needing to know that work schedules weren't dependent on your level of positive energy. Self-care and aligned chakras don't care about bills.

"But Deena and Amory talked about this place so much, I thought, what could it hurt? I was getting burned out in the city. My friends thought I was insane when I mentioned I was moving to Montana."

"Not the place you'd think would welcome the LGBTQ community."

"I mean, it's not perfect here, but nowhere is. I like the quiet. Cost of living makes it where I don't have to kill myself to pay my bills, which I was working two jobs before coming here and couldn't pay my rent without two roommates. Best of all, I can still be me from the makeup to my high heels. What about you? I know your dad owned the store before you. As many lunches as we've shared, you're not too open with information."

"Oh, Dad took over from my grandfather who opened it a few years before my dad was born. It was a family tradition. My wife wasn't...let's just say she found me boring. After high school, I went away for college but always intended to come home, we'd get married, and I'd take over the store. She thought since my dad passed away right after I graduated college, I'd have no more ties to Jenkins, and we'd leave."

"She didn't know you very well. You're a staple in this town."

"I don't drink. Bars don't hold a fascination for me. My mom and dad were together until she passed away from breast cancer when I was ten, and he never remarried. He was still completely in love with her as much as he'd been in high school. I guess I wanted that. It just didn't work out that way."

"Her loss. Sure I can't talk you into dinner? I even stopped at the store before I came home."

"No, I'm fine. I need to get my horses in, fed, and brushed down for the night. Thanks for the coffee, though."

"Well, raincheck, maybe? The least I can do for a handsome man coming to my rescue."

"I'm sure you don't need rescuing. We help each other in this town."

"Just because I don't need it, doesn't mean it's not nice occasionally."

"I'll just get the other fire going and be on my way." I finished the dark brew and set the mug on the counter next to the sink.

I didn't feel as if I ran away, but I didn't enjoy talking about myself. He was from the city. I'm sure going out for drinks was normal for him. I was a simple man. I'd even thought maybe I'd meet a woman who'd spark my interest. A woman who didn't mind the life I led or that I had no intention of ever leaving Jenkins. I required little in my life.

After I got the fire going, I made sure he had everything he needed, and he walked me to the door. On my way home, I had to admit it was nice to have someone to talk to. I wasn't afraid to admit I was lonely; I just didn't know how to let people in.

2

SHUG

Wʜᴇɴ I ᴍᴏᴠᴇᴅ ᴀᴡᴀʏ ғʀᴏᴍ ʜᴏᴍᴇ ғᴏʀ ᴀ ǫᴜɪᴇᴛᴇʀ ʟɪғᴇ, I'ᴅ made a promise that I would find the one man for me and settle down into a nice life. Over a hundred dates later, I've struck out once again. Bad thing was I drove an hour to spend thirty minutes with a man who apparently didn't read my profile just looked at my picture. Hell, by this point, I'd take a good deep stroke dicking and call it a fucking win.

I hadn't been abstinent since I learned that sex was fun and almost as good as masturbation. People would say I was crazy, but if people practiced enough, everyone could ring their own bell perfectly. I pulled to the side of the deserted road back into town and leaned my head back against the seat.

My mother was in Poly or open relationships my entire life until the current incarnations of her soulmates arrived a year ago. Why all her soulmates looked like *Grateful Dead* rejects, I did not know, but whatever made her happy. I just wanted one decent man who could keep it in his pants for everyone but me and wasn't emotionally unavailable. How could those require- ments be too high on the standards list?

A knock on my window had me jerking my head up and

just what I needed to see through the glass: Grey. I hit the button to put the window down.

"Car problems?"

I almost lied because it would save me a bit of pride, but the man was too nice, so he'd want to work on my non-broken car to be the nice, straight man he is. "No, dating issues."

"Are you okay?" The concern was clear in his baritone.

"Not really. How hard is it for someone to put *No Fats, No Femmes* in their dating profile before I drive an hour to have one watered-down drink? I bet he put it there now."

"Want some tea?"

"Got any whiskey?" I knew he didn't drink, but maybe he had an emergency bottle hidden away somewhere.

"I don't drink."

I groaned loudly, and he had the nerve to chuckle in that annoyingly sexy way he had. "You were perfect until then, but I guess tea would be nice. I *am* all dressed up and nowhere to go."

"About a mile ahead, there's a mailbox, turn in, and I'll meet you at the house."

"I can give you a ride."

"Rufus needs to be brushed and put away first."

I glanced over one very broad shoulder to a huge gray horse behind him. That's when I noticed his shirt was unbuttoned enough to show off a portion of his hairy chest, and he had his sleeves rolled up to expose arms that would be worthy of forearm porn. In the years I'd secretly lusted after the older, reserved man, he'd never had more than one button undone on his shirts or his sleeves rolled up. With skin uncovered, he was close to causing a scandal.

"I'll meet you at home then."

"The doors unlocked, so just let yourself in."

I nodded as he straightened and I put my car in drive, making the short trip to his place. A two-story house sat about a mile off the road. There were rocking chairs and even a porch swing. Across the yard to the left was a large barn and paddock with another horse; this one, a beautiful midnight color—almost blended into the shadows. I parked next to Grey's truck and slowly got out; the lights were on, and I carefully walked up the stone path to ascend the steps.

I felt weird letting myself into his home, but I removed my long jacket and hung it from a line of hooks beside the door. I wasn't nosy by nature, but I checked out his place. The floors were shiny yet battered dark hardwood. My heels clicked almost too loudly in the serene environment. His house was what you'd consider a family home, lived in and well-loved.

The furniture was dark brown leather, there was a woman's touch around the place, but you could tell one didn't live there. It was almost too neat and minimalistic. His style was the exact opposite of my chaotic, too colorful one. If two people could be more different, they would hold him and me as the supreme example.

I nervously wrung my hands and glanced down at them to take in the dark purple metallic polish on my nails. I wore black leather pants, an eggplant-colored dress-shirt with several open buttons, and the purple and silver loosely knitted scarf. To him, I probably looked ridiculous, but he'd never made me feel that way.

My perusal of the downstairs ended in the kitchen, and I looked around for what I needed to start the tea. I didn't know how long it took to get horses ready for the night but making tea was the least I could do for him letting me invade his space. Rumors were Grey was extremely private.

"You didn't have to do that."

I spun on my toes to find him almost filling the entryway of the kitchen. With my heels on, we were almost eye to eye, so I'd say he was a few inches over six foot, maybe six-three at the most, but he was strong and broad-shouldered. He was like the poster image for a sexy country boy. He was a man who didn't spend hours in a gym to stay in shape or hundreds of dollars on haircuts to look naturally mussed. The man was dangerous to my peace of mind; had been since the minute I'd walked into his hardware store the week I'd moved to Jenkins.

"I didn't know how long you'd be. I figured I'd get the water started."

"Thank you. What happened on your date, or don't you want to talk about it?"

I knew if I told him I didn't want to talk about my date, he wouldn't pry, but strangely I'd always felt a sense of safety and comfort in his presence. He was strong and dependable.

"I made this list of things I wanted to accomplish with the move. My own business. Independence. Being able to adult like a normal person."

"That doesn't explain the date," he stated as he passed me to grab a teapot and a canister of tea as the kettle whistled.

I did the weirdest thing I'd ever done; I inhaled the scent of the outdoors and subtle hints of a cologne that had probably worn off over the course of his day. I didn't make a habit of sniffing handsome, straight men. "Patience, my good man. I've marked just about everything on my list off. Finding the man for me is the last of my adult to-do list. In the last five years, I've gone on over a hundred dates, blind ones, and taking advantage of those dating apps. Every one of them has been a bust."

"Why?" He swirled hot water in the teapot and then filled it with more water.

I watched his big, scarred hands. I swore he was going to be my downfall. Never once in my thirty-one years had I ever lusted after a straight man. It had become a habit to break a lot of my personal rules. But this man screamed Daddy, and I wanted him all for myself. He had this strength that he just effortlessly exuded. Caring for others was natural for him. It was in the way he came to my house to fix my heat. All the stories I'd heard of him volunteering his time to act as handyperson so no one had to pay money they didn't have to maintenance people or whatever.

"I don't know, just like with any demographic in the world, gay men have a preference."

"Oh, the fat and femme thing you mentioned." He motioned to the small table in the corner of the room.

I took a seat, and he followed, setting the table and added a plate of cookies. "Yeah, men see my profile picture, and well, the carefully cultivated five o'clock shadow, my size, makes it look like I'm butch, which is far from the reality."

"Just because you like pretty things and wear the occasional skirt, I'm sure you'd be a catch." He poured tea over a strainer he placed on a delicate cup; I smiled my thanks as I added sugar as he prepared his own.

"If only most gay men thought the same, love. Even prejudice exists in marginalized communities."

"That's on them, not you, Shug."

"I try to remind myself, but after you go on so many disastrous dates, your pride and self-esteem gets a bit dinged up. And what makes you think I want to take dating advice from the biggest confirmed bachelor in town, maybe the state?"

His lips twitched at the corners. "What's the saying, those who can, do, those who can't, give advice."

"Close enough. You've broken a lot of hearts of the female population of Jenkins, maybe some males, too."

"I don't know about that. It's not that I wouldn't like to find someone, but you grow up in a small town, and you know most everyone. They're your friends, or at the very least a close acquaintance. Things could get awkward if it doesn't work out. Difficult to date when you know everything about everyone."

"Shouldn't that make it easier?"

"Probably, but I don't know. Like you said, I'm a confirmed bachelor. After my marriage fell apart, I had all the well-meaning ladies in town coming by to drop off casseroles and bringing daughters and granddaughters along to *introduce* us."

"Poor sought-after man that you are."

His chuckle was deep and husky. Maybe tea with him while alone in his house was a bad idea. Our shared lunches and social run-ins were always in a group, or possibly a customer would walk into his store. We were never truly alone.

"My life runs like clockwork. I get up at four every morning, I shower, make coffee and breakfast, take care of my horses, and then I'm turning the sign of the store at exactly six AM. Home by six-thirty, chores, dinner, and a book before bed. Get up the next day and do it all over again."

"You make it sound like there's something wrong with that."

"My ex-wife thought I was boring."

"Did you lie to her about what you wanted from life?"

"No."

"Then that's on her, not you."

"What are you looking for?"

I knew what I wanted but paused as if I were thinking about his question. "My mom and several friends have always had open or Poly relationships." I grinned at his scowl. "I'm too much of a diva to share. Mainly I just want a decent guy I can rely on. A man who doesn't require me to change myself." I hesitated as I locked gazes with him as he brought his cup to his perfectly formed lips. "A man who's a powerhouse in the bedroom wouldn't hurt either."

He snorted so hard that he choked on the tea he'd just taken a sip of and glared at me.

"Should I apologize for hot tea coming out of your nose?" I picked up a napkin and handed it to him, making sure my smile was sugary sweet and innocent. I didn't deny being a brat, and one thing about Grey was, he was easy to shock.

"Would it be sincere?"

"Nope." I made sure to draw it out and pop the P as I answered.

"Didn't think so."

"I better get home; you have to be up early." I finished my tea, and while I wanted to stay longer, it wasn't a good idea for my sanity to remain alone in his presence. Spending too much time with him always proved dangerous.

"Give me your phone." It's the first time I'd ever heard a demanding tone from him. He was always too polite.

"Why?"

"It's late and dark out, I want you to text or call me when you get home, or I can follow you to make sure."

"I'm a big boy. I can make it home just fine." I rolled my eyes as he held out his hand, and I leaned forward to pull my phone out of my back pocket. When I handed it over, he tapped the screen, and I heard a phone ringing from another room.

"Text or call. It'll make me feel better."

I took my phone back and stood. "I promise." Before I could think it over too much, I leaned down and pressed a kiss to his cheek and then used my thumb to scrub a bit of lipstick off his tanned, scruffy skin. "You're very much a catch, Grey. Why don't you put one of those ladies out of their misery? You're damned near perfect. You even make this jaded gay boy lose his mind a bit."

I backed away from the table and headed to the front door to collect my coat. As I was about to shrug into it, he took it from me, and I turned to slip my arms into it. I opened the door and stepped out onto the porch. I spun on my toes and smiled up at him.

"I promise, you'd have the ladies lined up from your door to town. Girls want excitement and bright lights, women know what they want, and you're a woman's dream come true."

As he opened his mouth to deny the truth in my words, I rushed for my car, trying to pretend like I wasn't running from him. A bottle of wine and some binge-watching awaited me. Didn't matter I wanted to run back up on the porch just to spend a bit more time with the unattainable Grey.

3

GREY

"Hey, man, you in here?"

My best friend, Drew's, voice came from the barn doors, and I looked up from where I was finishing putting down fresh hay.

"Yeah, what are you doing out this way?" I asked as I set the pitchfork aside and walked out of the stall.

"Didn't see you at the diner for breakfast. Came by to check on you."

He and I were opposites of each other. The respected attorney wore a designer sweater and jeans. His haircut cost more than I'd spent in three years total. He was one of those classy guys who was always comfortable in his own skin. How we'd stayed friends since we were kids, I did not know.

"I miss one Sunday, and you came looking for my dead body."

"You are a creature of habit. Everyone's talking about you being a no show."

I groaned and rolled my eyes. If I wasn't already hyper-aware of my love of a strict routine at that moment, I would've gotten reminded. That morning I'd awakened, and for the first time in years, I hadn't wanted to get up. I'd spent a lot of time alone and left too much time to reflect. I was coming up on forty. Was that too early for a midlife crisis? My brain wasn't thinking so.

"I'm sure when you go back to town and have dinner, you can spread the word I'm very much alive."

"I'll make sure I let the ladies know they still have you to lust over."

That was the second person to talk about me and the women lusting after me. Mine and Shug's conversation still played in my head days later. I didn't see myself as some ultimate catch. I was a passably attractive man who ran his family's hardware store. I had more flannel and denim in my wardrobe than any man needed. Comfort was all I wanted.

"You and Shug have a high opinion of my appeal."

"You hanging out with the pretty man more now?"

"He had a shitty date the other night, and he pulled over to the side of the road to have a breather. I was out riding and spotted him. We had tea and talked for a bit. Is there a rule somewhere the straight guy can't have multiple gay male friends?"

He laughed loudly. "If you don't remember, I'm bi. That means…"

"I know what it means, smartass."

I walked back into the stall and grabbed the pitchfork to return it to the storage room. The horses wouldn't come back in until sunset for some feed and a brushing. I'd probably spoiled them with all the attention, but after my dad passed, I'd sold off the small herd of cattle, and a rescue took the older horses, but I kept the younger ones. The thought of being a rancher, even on a small scale, hadn't interested me.

"You okay? You've been weirder than normal lately."

"Yeah, I'm fine." I closed the storage room door, and we headed up to the house. "I just didn't feel like getting up this morning." I held the door for him, and once he grabbed it, I made my way to the kitchen and the fresh pot of coffee I'd started before I went out to do chores.

"Like I said, weird. Four AM, you hit the floor running. I've always assumed you were a pod person who got left on Earth by some alien overlords."

"You and Shug are comedians." I poured us both coffees, took mine black and left him to doctor his with copious amounts of sugar and creamer.

Leaned back against the counter, I sipped at the strong brew and waited out his silence. I knew there was something on his mind. I also knew I just needed to be patient. He rarely came by without calling. I grinned at him every time he glanced in my direction and arched a brow in question. It earned me several eye rolls.

We knew each other's quirks. We used to double date in high school. My dad would drive me to pick up whatever girl I was dating, and the person Drew was seeing. Dad had even had a talk with Drew's parents when they'd threatened to throw him out. Showed up at his house and told Drew to pack his things, and he'd lived with us for six months before Drew's parents started acting right, and Dad had allowed him to move back home.

"So..."

"So, something on your mind, Drew?"

"There're some rumors going around town."

"If the people in this town know how to do anything, it's gossip. Who's the target this time?"

"You."

I groaned. "I missed one damn breakfast. It's not the end of the world."

"They noticed you at Shug's house a few weeks ago."

Shrugging my shoulders, I wondered what me going to a friend's house had to do with rumors. "His furnace went out. I went by to see about fixing it for him before he had to spend any money. You know Mrs. Peterson didn't keep up with the maintenance on the house. I sent a friend over to replace it."

"Heard you covered the labor so Shug wouldn't have to pay for it."

I grumbled; I didn't want that getting back to Shug. "Don't let that slip to him. He'll come stomping over in those high heels of his to get all huffy. But what does that have to do with rumors about me?"

"They've been wondering if they should start introducing their sons and grandsons instead of their daughters and grand-daughters."

I let out a loud laugh and shook my head. "My best friend is bi, has been since we were in grade school. Wouldn't the gay rumors have made the rounds before Shug moved to town?"

"I'm just saying what I heard. He amuses you."

"Of course, he does. He's a nice guy. A bit high-strung, and he's fun to be around. Also, it's easy to bring out his diva tendencies."

He had that appraising expression again; the suspicion made me nervous about what was really going on.

"You're not bothered people are thinking the formerly confirmed straight bachelor is smiling at the adorable Shug?"

"Why would I be? People can think what they want about me. Mom and Dad weren't bigoted people. I won't stop being friends with him because the town suddenly thinks I'm gay by association."

"That's not what I meant. I don't care who you do or don't date, but you've been extra reclusive since the divorce. Suddenly, he has you doing repairs at his shop and house. He makes you smile. The rumors aren't bad. You know that. Jenkins' residents aren't like that. Admit he's pretty."

"He is. I'm not mired in toxic male bullshit. I have no problem admitting someone is attractive, no matter their gender. You have an interest in Shug?" I tried to sound casual as I asked, but I was conflicted about Drew taking an interest in Shug.

Drew was a nice guy, but he wasn't ready to settle down. From what Shug had told me the other night, he wanted to find a man to have a relationship with, and that wasn't my best friend. I wasn't even sure what he wanted out of life, but he didn't like being tied down. The few long-term relationships he'd had always ended amicably and by mutual agreement.

"No, I don't have an interest in him. He's a bit too high-maintenance for me."

"Two high-strung people can't be in a relationship?"

"I am not high-strung."

He might not think so, but his indignant squeak said otherwise. "Oh, you so are, my friend. I remember your first zit."

"I was thirteen."

"You made me get all your assignments for two days. Let's not forget your first gray hair. You acted like your life was over."

"I was twenty-eight, and you telling me you thought you saw a bald spot forming was not nice."

I snorted at the horror on his face. "You have more skin care products than people need."

"I'm not ruggedly handsome, Grey. I'm not built like some cowboy or country boy centerfold. I look at a cookie, and my waistline expands. You haven't worked out in your life except for when you were playing football and not a sign of middle-age spread. You're not human."

"Can't hate me for good genes."

"Oh, Carlos' birthday is Saturday. We're meeting up at Shane's. He wants you to come."

"You know I don't drink."

That was always my go-to excuse when someone wanted me to attend functions where having a drink would be expected. I had nothing against a drink or two. Although, in college, I'd done more than my share and hadn't liked the feeling of being out of control. For two years, I'd partied after Brenda and I parted ways for college, not feeling ready for a long-distance relationship. We'd done our own thing during our break, and more out of familiarity than anything, we did what our parents expected when we returned to Jenkins.

"Going to a bar doesn't mean you have to drink. You have friends who'd like to hang out with you. One night out may be painful for the old-before-his-time persona you have going, but it won't kill you. Shug will be there."

"Your clumsy attempts at setting up your straight best friend with a gay man..."

"I'm not setting up, but you'll have fun. He's always the life of the party."

"I'll think about it."

"Man, you know I love you. You've been my best friend for longer than I want to admit, but one clusterfuck of a marriage doesn't mean you can't meet another nice girl to settle down with and have a family. Everyone knows how your parents and grandparents were. You have a legacy of powerful love stories. Brenda wasn't a fit for you. We all knew. It just took you a decade after exchanging vows to figure it out."

"What do I have to offer?"

"You're a nice guy. Successful. You're a gentleman, but I'm sure there's a freak of immense proportions hiding under that buttoned-up old-fashioned façade you give off. And as long as you've been without sex, some lucky lady will benefit from years and years of pent-up, unsatisfied lust."

Hell, even being married hadn't satisfied that. Brenda hadn't enjoyed sex with me, and I wouldn't ask when I knew she would only do it out of duty. I wondered if people knew she was seeing someone for the last four years of our marriage. Bad thing was, I hadn't cared, and she knew. There just hadn't been a reason to change my life when her cheating didn't bother me.

"Maybe I'm a missionary position with the lights out kinda guy." I winked at him, which set him off chuckling.

"No wonder you're divorced."

"Hey, be nice to the old, jaded man."

"Yeah, yeah. Be at Shane's at eight Saturday night. Leave two buttons undone on your shirt. You'll scandalize the entire town."

I kicked him out and made more coffee. Just like the old, jaded man I was, I sat down on one of the rockers on my porch and stared out at acres of land, forest, and mountains in the distance. There were a few times over my life I'd toyed with the idea of selling it all and moving away. Finding a new town or small city where I could open a store and find someone who knew nothing about me. I'd even talked to a real estate agent and almost listed the land and store for sale. Yet looking back, I couldn't see myself leaving. I loved this town and my home.

Maybe Drew was right, and I needed to try again. One awful marriage didn't make me unlovable, or at least I didn't think it did. I was too overbearing and set in my ways; I enjoyed opening doors and doing all those gentlemanly things people considered old-fashioned. I was affectionate, a tactile person, and wore out my welcome quickly. I just wanted someone to love and love on. Why the hell was that so hard to find?

4

SHUG

I LAUGHED AND DANCED AS ANOTHER DRINK FOUND ITS WAY into my hand. Carlos had called me during the week and told me his husband was throwing him a party at Shane's, the only strictly Queer establishment in town. The other two bars were mixed. It had seemed like a great idea; I needed something because I'd felt off after my aborted date.

The drink in my hand earned a glare, and I was planning on where to get rid of that one. Usually, I wasn't averse to a buzz and some dancing, but I wanted to go home to my silk pajamas and the new romances I'd downloaded to my e-reader earlier that day. Since I couldn't find romance in the real world, I'd thought reading about happily ever afters would be good enough.

When did I become so cynical?

A rousing echo of *Cheers*-like greetings turned my attention to the door and Drew coming through, and then a wider male frame entered right behind him. Like always, my lips tugged into a smile, but I quickly hid it by pretending to take a sip of the fruity drink.

Carlos had mentioned he'd invited Grey and had put Drew in charge of getting him there. I hadn't prepared myself to see him since he wasn't a drinker or the type for crowds. Drew broke through the circle of people to give Carlos a hug and a loud kiss on the cheek, and I stepped back to allow room. Si, Carlos' husband, was possessive, and I would not be caught in some testosterone-driven Neanderthal crossfire.

A big hand spread over the small of my back, and I tilted my head back slightly to find Grey smiling at me.

"Is two minutes too short before saying my goodbyes?" he asked and widened his eyes in mock panic.

"That would be exceptionally rude. Find a corner and post up to hide."

"I knew there was a reason I liked you. You're a genius."

I leaned toward the bar and ordered a bottle of water. I took it when the bartender handed it over and then straightened to hold it out for Grey.

"Thanks." He took his turn greeting Carlos.

I rolled my eyes as I watched Carlos' hands lower to the muscular curves of Grey's perfect ass, and I made a dramatic show of moving them upward to Grey's lower back. That earned me a wink from Carlos. I knew people speculated about my intentions toward Grey. A few of my friends even called me out on my crush and how useless it was to lust after the straight man, but except for that one enormous obstacle, the off-limits man was just what I wanted in a boyfriend, partner or whatever.

The heart wants what the heart wants, or however the saying goes.

"Hands off my husband, you handsome bastard." Si playfully broke Carlos and Grey apart.

"Wasn't me doing the groping," Grey muttered but gave the tipsy Carlos a wink.

"Shug, watch him." Si pointed at Grey.

"I didn't come to babysit, and he's big enough to take care of himself."

"Do as I say," Si ordered.

"Fine, should I find him a blanket so no one can be tempted by his chiseled perfection?" I put on my best innocent expression and looped my arm through Grey's, pulling him away from the crowd. "I need to find somewhere to hide this drink," I announced when we were out of the crowd.

"Not in a party mood? My cranky ways aren't rubbing off on you, are they?" I snorted, and he gave me a gentle shake. "Of course, you'd have a gutter mind. How many drinks have you had?"

"Technically two, four of them I ditched. Maybe I'll just hang onto this one. That way, no one buys me anymore. How did Drew get you here?"

"Told me a night out wouldn't kill me."

"Didn't tell you you'd get felt up two minutes after walking in the door."

"It's Carlos's birthday, whatever makes him happy."

"You're a very weird man."

He took my hand, and with his free one, pulled out a chair for me at a table away from the crowd. Few men I met were gentlemanly. I sensed it wasn't something he consciously did. It was his nature to open doors, pull out chairs, and just to be overall nice to everyone. Part of me always thought I was too independent to go for that nice pampering type of man, but as I grew older and then met Grey, I was way more than intrigued. I wasn't averse to a dominant man in the bedroom, and the idea brought on thoughts of the other times I wondered what Grey was like behind closed doors, especially the bedroom one.

"I'm hearing that a lot lately." He settled himself onto the chair beside me and leaned his forearms on the table, rolling his bottled water between his palms.

I took in the twin lines between his thick brows as they deepened as if he was worried about something. He was too stoic and laid back to wear that expression. We were friends. Not until the last few years did we hang out more than it took to order something from his store or pick it up, maybe the occasional lunch when I was too weak to ignore my attraction. The distance I put between us was more about keeping my heart safe than anything. I wanted to soothe his discomfort, though. I had to remind myself it wasn't my place; he didn't belong to me. "How's that?"

"Drew said I was acting weird and more reclusive than normal."

"Nothing wrong with enjoying your quiet and alone time. I've been thinking about the books I downloaded before I forced myself to leave my house. I'll be thirty-two next month. Maybe I'm hitting middle-age."

"I'll be forty next year. We can have mid-life crises together."

"Does that mean we can sit on a porch in our rockers and yell at pesky kids to get off our lawns?" I quickly nudged his bicep with my shoulder and then straightened. Less contact would be a great idea. As I touched him, I enjoyed that he was broadly built, not gym fit but a man who worked to keep in shape. He was solidly cuddly, and he'd be scared to know how much I dreamed of snuggling him and a lot of other stuff.

"You're not as funny as you think you are."

"Ouch, I've always been told I have a spectacular sense of humor." I planted my elbow on the table and rested my chin on my curled hand as I batted my lashes.

"Were all of those people friends?"

I gave a mock gasp. "You're just nasty tonight. I should've let Si kick your sexy ass."

"Now who's being nasty?" He leaned back and stretched his right arm along the back of my chair and seemed to survey the room.

"I know there are a few bi ladies in the crowd if you want introductions."

"No need for introductions. Like I said, I know everyone in this town. Besides, those two bi ladies in the crowd are interested in each other, but neither wants to make the move."

"In my experience, the women-loving-women crowd I know are pretty clueless about someone interested in them."

"Are we speaking stereotypes, Shug?"

"Love, I wouldn't do that. I don't care about sexuality. Some people are just naturally clueless about their appeal."

"Why do I sense we're not talking about lesbians, and you're being more specific?"

"You know half the single men in this room are eyeing you like they'd love to make a feast of you."

"And as I've mentioned countless times to Drew, it doesn't bother me. Finding another human attractive is natural, whether that's sexually or just in a sense of general appeal."

"Very philosophical of you."

"Don't let the rugged looks fool you."

I laughed at his rakish wink and grin and shook my head. "Why the hell are you single? I know you've explained before, but I don't get it."

"I told you. I'm boring, and women want excitement and spontaneity."

"Girls want those things. Women want someone who treats them well. Who they can count on. Maybe I should set you up on some blind dates." I schooled my features not to show my dislike of that idea, but the horror on his face made me feel better.

"No, I'm sure you'd do an amazing job, but no."

"Wow, you even turned me down politely. You, sir, are the mythical unicorn, the rare gentleman."

"I'm sure there's plenty out there, but what do they say? The nice guy always finishes last. People find the bad boy persona more attractive. It's the danger of it…a hint of the forbidden and unattainable."

"There could be another connotation for the nice guy finishes last, but I won't point that out."

"Wasn't that a roundabout way of saying it?"

"Perception, my good man. Okay, I'm going to suggest something completely radical. You'll have to bear with me."

"What?"

I didn't know why. Maybe it was pure selfishness on my part, or I was a glutton for punishment. "Undo a top button and cause a wave of people having the vapors." When he didn't move, I raised my hands and slipped two buttons free of their holes to expose thick, dark chest chair.

Shug, you will not pet the Bear, do not pet the Bear, Shug. Fuck, I wanted to pet the Bear.

"What are you doing?"

"Causing the scandal of the century, I'm mussing you."

He could've easily fought me off as I undid his cuffs and rolled the sleeves up over strong, furry forearms. A shiver threatened to overtake me when the fingers of first one hand then the other brushed the soft curve of my silk-covered belly. "Men in rolled-up sleeves on their dress-shirts, it's like modest but oh so dirty," I purred with a roll of my tongue as I finished and leaned back to survey my work. "One more thing." I finger-combed his hair to find the neatly combed strands easily tangled into sexy waves.

Oh fuck, that wasn't my best idea ever. I couldn't look away from that V of skin and hair exposed by his opened collar. I'd never thought I had a type before; I'd dated femme and masc, skinny and fat. I liked people, and I found the differences and imperfections attractive. Yet Grey was proving me wrong—I had a type. They were masculine, too handsome men with old-fashioned manners. No wonder I was perpetually single. My perfect man was straight.

"Do I pass muster?"

"I may need to fix you. You'll cause a riot." I darted a glance around to find men and women looking at him, and I started to reach for him to button his shirt and cover his forearms. His sex appeal was bad enough when he was completely covered. I wondered for the hundredth time what he looked like naked. What was he like when his usual civility disappeared behind closed doors?

"What the hell are you two doing hiding in a corner?" Drew fell onto my lap and wrapped his arm around my shoulders. Saved from embarrassment by a drunk man.

"We're not in a corner, honey. And how many shots have you had?" I asked as I took in his flushed face and heavy-lidded eyes.

"Shot relay, I don't remember."

I grimaced and shot a glance at Grey. I'd done a shot relay with Carlos last year, and I didn't remember how I got home the next morning. I know I didn't walk miles home on stilettos.

"I hope you got a ride here."

"I'll make sure he gets home safe, along with anyone else. I'm labeled *Designated Driver* in everyone's phone, and Shane knows to call me. I threw everyone in the bed of my truck last time."

Did the man have to be so fucking nice?

"I saw you two getting cozy. Stripping men is for private time, Shug."

I pinched Drew hard and earned a glare, but I didn't need anyone drunkenly vomiting up the rumors going around town. If he had already heard them, he was too polite to mention the fact to me. As attracted as I was to Grey, I loved having him as a friend. Maybe people saying that I had a thing for him would make him less comfortable around me, and I couldn't have that.

Questionable decisions when it came to men was my usual modus operandi. I loved intimacy and sex, even when the men I usually ended up sweaty in bed with would not keep me. Abstinence was frying my few remaining brain cells, but even when I saw the hurt coming, I still found myself helpless to say no.

5

GREY

As always, when the bell went off over the front door signaling a customer, I came out of the back where I'd spent most of the morning organizing the backroom. I was still paying for my four AM morning after Carlos's party. I'd made sure the attendees I took charge of made it home. Thankfully Shug had graciously—if with more than a little amusement—helped me with intoxicated and friendly partygoers. With every invite I'd received to come in, he'd cackled from the passenger seat where he watched me fight off several advances. I think they felt me up more than I'd been in a decade of marriage.

And who I didn't need to see walked in on a pair of dark purple stiletto thigh-high boots and a pair of black leggings with a peacoat over a baggy shirt. I glared at him, and he pursed his lips to hide a smirk. He didn't do a very good job.

"Oh, love, you look like shit."

"Thank you, Shug. Good afternoon to you as well." I spread my hands on the counter and rested my weight on them.

He smiled brightly, and his septum piercing glinted under the florescent lights. When he'd closed the last few feet between us, he rested his forearms on the battered surface and leaned in close.

"Aw, baby, you know, even looking like hell, you're still the sexiest man in this town."

"What are you up to?"

He gasped dramatically. "I'm hurt, love. What makes you think I didn't just want to come by to see your handsome face?"

The light-speed pace of his thick lashes caused the corners of my mouth to twitch. The man could be annoying as hell and still brightened a damn room. What the hell was that? Again, I was made aware of how different we were, and I wanted to interrogate him about why he wasted his time with me.

"You can't stay mad at me."

"Then you're just here to be a pain in the ass."

"Nasty, grumpy man. Maybe I just wanted to visit you on my lunch break."

Which wasn't impossible. He always closed his shop down between noon and one PM every day. But his extra flirty behavior made me suspicious.

"Grey?"

"Yes, Shug?"

He spun and looked over his shoulder. "Lift me."

I shook my head and circled the counter. By the widening of his eyes, he didn't think I'd take him seriously. I gripped his waist, my hands and fingers sunk into his soft curves, and I easily lifted him onto the counter. He had a body meant to be cuddled, and like him with me, I wondered why the hell the sweet man was single. His gloss-covered lips dropped open. A smirk tugged at the corners of my mouth, and I moved back to my position behind the counter.

A laugh threatened to escape as he sat there frozen, and then he seemed to realize what he was doing. Shug crossed his legs and turned slightly, and then he was looking at me. My opportunities to shock the outrageous man were almost nil until I picked him up. He may carry a bit of extra weight, but to me, he was just Shug. But a thought occurred to me that he may see himself differently. He was always so confident, and I was occasionally jealous of it.

"Comfortable?" I asked to break the silence because time with Shug never included quiet. He always had to fill something with chatter or noise.

"Did you hurt yourself? Dislocate a shoulder?"

"Shut up. You don't weigh a thing."

He snorted so hard he choked, and I sent him a glare. I almost opened my mouth to tell him I loved how he felt, but I refrained. That was crossing a line a straight man shouldn't step over.

"Love, I know what I look like and what I weigh."

"Whatever. Did you bring your lunch, or do I have to share with you?"

"I ordered. It should be here any minute. But on the off-chance I wish to steal some of your lunch, what did you make?"

"Quite boring, a couple of sandwiches and chips. I made a roast last night and sliced it for sandwiches."

"A man who cooks and has the strength of Superman, we have to find you a girlfriend."

I hid the snarl of my nose as I went to my office and grabbed my lunch bag. Most of the time, I didn't mind the talk of setting me up or the questions about when I was going to date again, but recently I'd realized it started to annoy me. Sometimes I wasn't happy with my solitary life. Yet, that didn't mean I had any impulse to change it. When I returned, the delivery guy was entering.

"Hi, Shug, Grey."

"Ansel, I'm starving."

Shug grabbed the paper bag and held it to his chest. Ansel set the to-go cup next to Shug's hip.

"You're always starving. My brother is a chef and only lives forty minutes away, he's recently single, but he's getting ready to date again."

My brows drew together at the attempt at a setup, and I didn't like something about it. "Ansel, how's the wife? That baby should arrive soon."

"A few more weeks, but we're thinking any time now. Our first was a few weeks early, too. I better get going, Bird is watching the shop while I do the lunch deliveries, and I hate to leave her alone."

The tension in my body didn't disappear until we were alone again. I watched Shug tear the bag open and start unpacking his fries and burger. He smacked my hand with fingers tipped with long silver nails as I tried to steal a fry from his lunch.

"Eat your healthy homemade lunch and leave my fries alone. This figure can't afford to lose a fry."

"You going to take Ansel up on the introduction?"

We ate in silence for a few minutes, and I noticed he was looking for a napkin. I pulled a few brown paper ones from under the counter. He smiled his thanks as he took them.

"I don't know, I mean, hell, it would be nice to meet some-one. Do all the dating things, get to know and first kisses, and all that, but—" He dropped his chin to his chest.

I placed my fingertips under his chin and raised his head until he looked at me. There was a strange emotion in his eyes I hadn't seen before, almost like sadness. His nearly black eyes were always filled with laughter and joy, occasionally surprise. "Come on, Shug, you're not the type to be lost for words." When I realized I wanted to stroke my thumb across his lower lip to test the plump curve, I dropped my hand back to the counter. Being lonely was frying my brain.

"I think I'm a lost cause."

"Bullshit."

"Profanity? Are you feeling okay?"

"Quit deflecting. What's really going on in your head?"

"I've never really had a type, you know. I've dated or slept with all types of men. A lot of people have preferences, and there's nothing wrong with that. We want what we want."

"This isn't about what other people want. What do *you* want?"

He picked at his food and wouldn't look at me.

"What I can't have. I met this amazing guy, but he's not available. I'll get over it."

"Maybe if he's ever available, you can ask him out, or someone better could come along." I hid my frown by taking a bite of my sandwich. The roast beef and the horseradish sauce I made was flavorless.

"Thanks, but this is peak unavailable. It's fine. We all get crushes on people. Speaking of crushes, how many numbers did you get Saturday night?"

I groaned as I let him change the subject. Him being sad wasn't something I could handle because that wasn't my friend. He always brought the light and positivity. His mission in life was to make sure everyone around him was smiling and laughing. It was one of the first things I'd noticed about Shug as I got to know him.

"None that I hadn't already had programmed into my phone. I think I have everyone in town's number."

"You weren't joking about being designated driver?"

I took a bite of my sandwich and watched as he moved half his fries to the wax paper I'd used to wrap my lunch.

"Nope. My dad used to do it, too. If the teenagers didn't feel safe calling parents to pick them up, Dad would pile them in the back of his truck. No questions. No judgment. Dad's best friend in high school drove home one night and didn't make it. He was only a mile away from his driveway when he passed out at the wheel. I remember him and Mom joking about all the calls that came in during the middle of the night. She once asked him did he have a girlfriend and the taxi service was just a cover."

He chuckled, and I felt better.

"I see the nice guy genes are strong in your family. Never thought about carrying on the family name?"

"Briefly, but when Brenda left, I was glad we hadn't had kids. She was on birth control, and I never forgot a condom."

"Seems overkill but knowing she was cheating probably a good idea."

"Those were my thoughts. What about you? Kids?"

"Oh no, I don't think I could do that. Mini versions of me running around? The clothes and nail budget alone would be staggering."

"Understandable, I see you went longer and silver for this week."

"I'm not feeling the longer nails, but there is something evil villainess about the ominous slow clicking of nails." He demonstrated and waggled his brows at me.

"Only you, Shug, only you."

"Love, don't make that sound like a bad thing."

"Never. Now, finish your lunch. If I remember correctly, you mentioned a tendency to be *hangry* if you don't eat."

"Aren't you sweet, looking out for me?"

I avoided him pinching my cheek, but I didn't mind him being slightly annoying as long as he was happy. The thought made me feel off, something I was getting used to with him. I treated him no differently than I did Drew. No matter how little time we spent together hanging out, I still considered him one of my best friends. There was something odd about it, though. I wished I could figure out what.

6

SHUG

"HI, SUGAR, HOW IS MY BEAUTIFUL CHILD TODAY?"

I smiled at my mother's voice. It was her weekly scheduled call to check in with me. Sometimes we played a lot of phone tag, so we'd made a deal for a weekly time to reconnect. Star was the only person to call me Sugar. After I'd gotten older, it had shifted to Shug. I'd asked her once why she named me Sugar out of all the other weird names she could've picked, and she'd simply said my black hair had looked like spun sugar. Could've been worse. Some kids I'd grown up with had gotten it bad.

"Hi. I'm good. How's things with the co-op?"

My mother and her partners ran a farmer cooperative where they paid fees by contributing to the free community garden where low-income and homeless could pick fruits and vegetables and have access to organic shelf-stable products.

She'd always surrounded herself with people who she claimed had peaceful auras. Growing up, I'd taken a lot of shit for who and what my mother was. We'd collected a family as we'd moved around the world. Most of the time, I hadn't noticed because my life was just, well, my life. It wasn't until we'd stopped the caravan in California, and I'd attended regular schools—that's where I'd learned nothing was normal about her or me.

"Amazingly well, we have a few new farmers that joined. Very positive vibes. Good people. Their auras are just so peaceful."

"That's great."

"I sense you're troubled."

"It's just the normal thing, Mom, I promise."

"From what you've told me, it's understandable to have fallen for him. And while I approve you found someone who brings you peace by being around him, it's not healthy to postpone our physical and spiritual sexual needs."

"You know people can have great intimate relationships without sex, right?"

"Yes, because I taught you that, Sugar. But denying ourselves touch and sex for those who require them isn't healthy. You know, sex is very important to you. You need that connection with someone, and your last three partners weren't good for you. Their energy was selfish, and that drained you, left you emotionally exhausted when you parted ways."

I stretched out on my bed because I knew this conversation would take a while. I'd never had to pay for therapy with a mom like her. "I'm working to get over my fascination with him. I think I'm just lonely and forming an attachment to distract myself from it."

"Is that true or just your way of trying to move me away from the conversation?"

I choked out a laugh at her almost bratty tone. For all my mother's aligned chakras and good vibes, she could be more annoying than me in the drama department. She really was one of those stereotypical hippies you saw on TV, barefoot and scenting of incense and weed. And she didn't care what people thought about her. Humans weren't meant to blend and fit. We were a unique blending of shades, shapes, spiritualities, and a thousand different variations. My upbringing was like an anthropologist's wet dream.

We lived in a world where we needed to fit. The survival of the fittest was still in play, but now it was more about money and popularity. Even at my age, I'd never learned to blend. After my nomadic life ended, whatever room or environment I walked into, I always stood out because of my clothes or personality. People were always nice to your face. Yet behind your back, they viewed you as the *Other*. I hated the emotions it elicited from me and the energy it drained of me. It was a double-edged sword—conformity or happiness? I couldn't possess both.

"Sugar?"

"Sorry, sorry, I was changing the subject. I just wonder if I were more the same, maybe life would be easier."

"It would, but where is the fun in that? We're inundated with sameness everywhere. Being judged by the clothing we wear, which should mean nothing more than keeping us cool or warm. Whether we shave when we naturally produce body hair for evolutionary reasons. The world can judge us on thousands of things, but will the conformity keep you warm at night or dry your tears when you cry? It may for a short time. Yet, bodies and people change. Age brings imperfections that tell our stories. Shows a life we lived with so many rewarding experiences. If we conform for the sake of societal safety, what do we really have?"

"Maybe a boyfriend that I don't wear out my welcome with or, in my current case, one who's actually gay."

"Everyone wants life to be easy when it's anything but."

"You're not being very helpful to your only blessed spawn."

"If I had always been helpful and normal, you wouldn't be as independent and perfect as you are."

"I thank you for that."

She let out a loud, husky laugh. "No you don't. I know you got hurt because of who I was."

"It wasn't your fault. I had an amazing childhood. Freedom that made other people jealous. I shouldn't have made that list." I didn't keep secrets from my mom. She knew everything about me, from when I lost my virginity to my stupidity over Grey. She never once judged me, except for that one time I tried to be popular back in high school with new off-the-rack mass-produced *boy* clothes and no makeup. She'd almost disowned me.

"Sugar, you've always walked your own path. There's never been one thing in your life you couldn't achieve."

I'd been lucky in life. I owned my store at twenty-six with a little financial help from my mother's trust fund from a long-deceased unconventional aunt, bought a home—professionally I couldn't complain about my life. My mother was right. I wasn't clueless about the clusterfuck my romantic life was.

"Maybe you should just mark that one thing off. Love doesn't happen on a timeframe. We can't say we're going to find our soulmate at a certain date or time. The blind dates and your apps haven't been working. Why not let Fate take control on this one? Maybe the saying about finding love when we least expect it could work for you."

"True. I could've latched onto the unattainable to sabotage myself."

"I won't say that's the case, but you've never fallen for a straight man before."

She was right. I hated she was, though. Thankfully, the rest of our weekly talk was more about her, her partners, and catching up with some of my friends that kept in touch with her. My friends and I had seemed to part ways when I moved. We exchanged calls and emails, mainly our interaction was strictly likes and comments on social media.

I'd made amazing friends since I'd moved here. I had a fulfilling social life, but it was no longer about clubs. No, I went out to small-town gay bars and brunch on Sundays with my married friends. Jenkins had opened a full range of new experiences for me. The people were more like the ones I'd grown up with, eclectic and laid back. It wasn't all about what you were wearing or where you were seen.

Too soon, we ended our conversation, and I reluctantly said goodbye and told her I loved her. I tossed my phone on my nightstand and stood up, and then I made my way to the kitchen. There was a well-stocked freezer with all the ice cream I could want. I opened it and pulled out the one with the most chocolate, grabbed a spoon, and walked into my living room. I curled my legs under me and held my silk robe together.

I found some mindless romantic comedy I'd seen a hundred times just because I knew it had a happily ever after. My depressive mood probably had far more to do with my upcoming birthday than anything. Another year of being single. I'd never had an issue with my figure. I loved the softness of my body, but sometimes it was hard to find a bed partner. I thought it would be easier being away from image-obsessed California, but that hadn't been the case.

When I moved here, I'd heard all the stories about how welcoming the community was, but the cynic in me remained skeptical. I'd quickly gotten over it the first week in town, and then I'd needed paint for my new house. I'd walked into Grey's hardware store, and the most handsome man I'd ever seen stood tall behind the counter. His niceness had knocked me for a loop. The crush had formed, but it wasn't until a few years later that I realized I liked the man a lot more than I should have.

For three years, we'd had this amazing friendship, I could be myself, and I didn't have to hide my personality or my flirty nature with him. He didn't get offended by me. All I could think about was what it would be like to kiss him. Every smile or smirk I earned made me want it more.

I angrily shoveled ice cream into my mouth and tried to push thoughts of him away, attempting to focus on my movie.

It was time to grow up and get over this stupid crush of mine. Yet the thought of putting distance between us killed me. If I couldn't have him, at least I could spend time with him. I'd spent the last few years keeping my hands to myself. I could continue to do so, and maybe one day, I'd find my one that wasn't Grey.

7

GREY

"COME ON, MAN, IT'S ONE NIGHT. YOU DON'T EVEN HAVE TO consider it a date. I've been waiting nearly a month for him to have time." Drew was close to begging.

To be honest, he didn't do this to me often. The few dates I'd been on that he'd set up hadn't been horror shows, but I also hadn't had a spark with any of them. I didn't want to go out at all. I'd just taken care of my horses and was checking my fridge for something to make for dinner.

"I didn't want to put it off. His best friend came to town without calling first. She said she didn't mind if he went, but he didn't want to leave her alone. All I could think to say was I had a friend."

"How long do I have to get ready?" As soon as the question was out of my mouth, he was across the kitchen and loudly kissing my cheek.

"An hour until we have to be at The Orchard. He agreed to come to Jenkins because of the change of plans. Luckily, Orchard had a few reservations. There's a party there tonight."

I was walking towards the stairs. "A party?"

"Yeah, didn't you know?"

I stopped on the bottom step as I took in his confused expression. "Why would I know?"

"It's Shug's birthday. I told him I couldn't come because I had a date, but then I realized it was at The Orchard. I told him I'd stop to give him a birthday spanking if he was a good boy."

"What?" I didn't know if that question was about not knowing it was his birthday or Drew thinking he was going to put his hands on Shug.

"Oh, man, you really didn't know?"

"No."

"Maybe it's because he didn't want you to feel out of place if they were drinking."

"But I went to Carlos's birthday, why wouldn't I go to Shug's?" I frowned as I continued up the steps with Drew on my heels as I tried to find a good reason for Shug not to invite me. The last few years, he'd been out of town for a few days to visit his mom around that time, but I didn't think it had anything to do with it being his birthday.

I didn't even get him a present or anything. Shit, he's going to be pissed at me. What could I do to make up for it?

"Don't worry about it. I'm sure he's okay. I don't think it was a big party or anything, just dinner and some drinks. You're going to be there tonight…you can wish him a happy birthday. It won't be a big deal."

"I didn't get him anything." That irrationally irritated me, and I was going through my closet looking for something date-appropriate while cursing myself. "What should I wear?"

"That baby blue dress-shirt looked great on you."

"The one I wore to Carlos's birthday?"

"Yeah, and leave some buttons undone and roll up the sleeves. You can wear your navy peacoat. You know ties aren't required."

"I'm feeling like an asshole right now. He's going to know I forgot his birthday."

"Get over it. It's not like he's your boyfriend or anything. He probably won't even notice."

I flinched at his tone. I knew that him and this guy he wanted to go out with had played phone tag for over a month. His frustration was getting the better of him. Shug and I were friends. I searched for a time he'd told me when his birthday was, hell, if anyone mentioned it. We'd known each other for five years; this was information I should've known, especially since he remembered mine. He always brought me a cupcake with a candle into the store. If the date fell on the weekend, he always came the Friday before to make sure I had my wish and a little present.

"You're right. I'll buy him lunch or something next week." I grabbed a pair of navy slacks, the shirt he said to wear, and a pair of dark brown distressed dress shoes. Shug had helped me pick them out for some wedding I had to go to a few years ago.

I disappeared into my bathroom to change, brushed my teeth, and tamed the waves of my hair. I swore I could hear every heavy sigh coming through the door as Drew paced outside of it. If he didn't want to wait, he should've called, but he knew I'd tell him no if he didn't beg in-person. I left the top button and two below it undone and adjusted it several times, uncomfortable about the amount of chest hair on display. Brenda had considered me too hairy. There was a time where I even shaved it because the women I'd dated or hooked up with didn't seem to like it. That had just made it grow back in thicker after. I'd stopped all that personal grooming I'd been strong-armed into once college was over.

I'd beat myself up later over my screw-up. Getting through this double date was going to be punishment enough. As I stepped out of the bathroom, Drew attacked me with my coat and pushed me out of my room and down the stairs. I barely had time to grab my phone and wallet out of the bowl on the foyer table.

"Slow down. It's not like a double date is going to end with sex. I can still change my mind."

"I will hogtie you and shove you in my damn truck. This is a nice guy. I'm not thinking about the date ending in fucking."

"You really like this one?" I asked as I opened the passenger door of his car.

"Yeah. We've talked or exchanged messages for over a month. I mean, there's been some dirty calls and flirting. The chemistry is there, but I need a date to find out if it's real. You can't really tell after sharing a table at a coffee shop because the place is packed."

"Fine, I'll do my best to entertain his friend."

"Thanks." He hit the button start on his car and turned around to head for the main road.

WALKING INTO THE ORCHARD, I INSTANTLY SPOTTED SHUG. If I hadn't seen him, I would've heard his voice and laugh. That sound always had a way of making me smile. I heard Drew saying we'd wait at the bar until the rest of our party arrived. Leaving him behind, I headed for the private room, and as I walked through the entryway, I spotted Shug.

He was holding court. He wore a black dress-shirt with ruffles down either side of the buttons, a tight dark red skirt that fell to just below his knees, dark tights, and a pair of ankle boots with his favorite dangerous heels.

"Grey," he yelled and waved his arms and walked out of the group. His dark eyes were glassy.

"How many of those did you have?" I looked at the martini he had in his hand.

"It's my birthday. I lost count."

"Happy birthday, Shug. You look beautiful." I wrapped my arms around his waist and gave him a hug and kissed his stubbly cheek. I frowned as he seemed to hold on when I tried to retreat, and his long nails played with the hair at the back of my neck.

When he seemed to pull away from me too quickly, I gripped his sides and studied his face, the way he wouldn't look at me. I hated when he'd mentally and emotionally lock me out. He didn't do it enough that I'd call him on it, but right then, I felt more concerned than annoyed.

"You okay? Do I need to take you home?"

"No, no, I'm sure—"

"Our dates are here, Grey."

I cursed Drew when Shug put even more distance between us. I dropped my arms to my sides. My hands curled into fists, but I forced myself to relax them.

"Shug, happy birthday. Looks like you're having fun."

"I was…I mean I am. Si promised to pour me into bed safe and sound, but Si has a very handsome friend in town. I might be lucky and get some birthday D."

I studied the group of people behind Shug to search out a stranger. There was one face I didn't recognize. He had that pretty look men and women seemed to like. Model perfect. "Maybe we can join the party and celebrate your birthday." I ignored the hard nudge of an elbow into my ribs but shot Drew a warning glare.

"No, no, Grey, your first date in a long time, I'm not messing that up. Go, go, have fun."

I didn't like the way he dismissed me. He'd never done it before. Shug always made time for me when we met up. We'd go to a corner or find a quiet spot to talk. I felt the furrows in my brow deepen as he drained the almost full glass and yelled at someone to bring him another.

"Shug, look at me." I waited until his eyes met mine and his open expression disappeared again. "I can take you home."

"And I said I'm fine. Don't let the skirts fool you. I'm a big boy, Daddy."

"Don't try that shit with me, Shug. I will carry you out of here, and you know I can do it."

"Grey," Drew called my name as he grabbed my arm. "He's an adult. He said he was fine. Let's go."

"Thanks for stopping by. Have fun on your date. I want details on Monday at lunch." He backed up, almost stumbling, and I rushed forward to catch him, but he righted himself.

He turned his back on me and returned to his group of friends.

"He's going to be fine. He's had a few too many, but you know Si will make sure he makes it home."

"Sure, yeah." I let Drew drag me away, but when we got to the table, I took the opposite side of the table that faced the room Shug was in so I could watch him.

As much as I liked and trusted Si, there was a stranger there who would take Shug home and take advantage. I wouldn't let that happen. I stood as Drew's date and his friend arrived. She was a beautiful blonde in a dress that left nothing to the imagination. Her hair was up in some elegant twist, and from her gaze sweeping my form, she liked what she saw. I vaguely heard Drew introducing us.

"Grey, it's lovely to meet you."

"You too, Margo." On autopilot, I pulled out her chair and then took mine. The server arrived, and I greeted the familiar young woman.

"You want your usual, Grey?" Usually, I had coffee, but I'd already had way more than I needed.

"No, I'll take a water and an iced tea."

"You're not going to have a drink?" she asked after she ordered a vodka martini.

"I don't drink." My tone clear I wouldn't be talked into one.

I didn't know what it was about saying you don't drink that made people want to talk you into it. It's one reason I didn't go out. If I was somewhere with Shug, he'd order me a water, and most everywhere I went, they knew I didn't partake in alcohol.

I darted a glance at Drew to find him staring at me, and his expression warned me to be nice. When hadn't I ever acted nice? I was always the nice guy. That didn't mean during dinner and dessert—that the lady didn't have—I wasn't sneaking glances into the private room to make sure Shug was okay.

My irritation grew, and I couldn't control it as I saw the stranger leaning in to whisper something in Shug's ear. Shug's cheeks darkened, either from what he said or from the drinks he was having. I'd tried to keep count. My mood wasn't getting better by pretending I was interested in what my date was talking about or the fact she kept touching me. At one point, I had to force a smile as she placed her hand on my knee, and I politely lifted it to put her hand on the table. Afterward, her attitude turned cold, and that was fine with me.

We were getting ready to pay the tab when Shug's party started filing out of the room. Si was getting ready to pass me, and I grabbed his arm.

"You're making sure he gets home, right?"

"My friend is giving him a lift."

"Simon, you're taking him home. Do not even dare let him get in the car with him. Do you understand me?" My tone was rough. It earned me an odd look, but Si had the sense to nod his head. The anger in my tone wasn't me. I didn't get mad; it didn't matter what happened. It's the reason most people thought I was too cold and emotionless, but if I found out that bastard got his hands on Shug, I'd destroy him.

"I won't."

"Text me when you get him inside." It wasn't a request. If I had to make Drew drive by Shug's house to make sure a strange car wasn't outside, I would.

"Okay. As soon as I make sure he's locked his door."

I nodded and released Si's arm, earning a few more strange looks from Si and Carlos. My hand wrapped around my water glass and saw my knuckles turn white by my grip. Our time together wasn't over soon enough, and I kept my usual polite façade in place, but I was ready to go home.

This wasn't me, I didn't get angry over nothing, but I was protective of Shug. He'd had too much to drink. And while Si knew the man, I didn't, and I didn't trust him to worry about consent. My friend didn't deserve that. He didn't need to be just a body for someone. Shug wanted a partner, a man to settle down with; to build a life.

I quickly said my goodbyes and headed for Drew's car to wait; I checked my phone to see a text from Si. Him and Carlos had to help Shug to bed, but they'd made sure he was okay and tucked in. I replied my thanks and apologized if I was an asshole. His last text said it was fine and that he understood. Hell, I wish I did.

The excessive drinking wasn't like Shug. There was that one time he'd done a shot relay with Carlos and I'd had to take him home, but he was normally someone who just got a little buzz to relax and nothing more. My friend was affectionate with me, and when he'd pulled away, it had hurt my feelings a bit. Something was wrong with me, and I just couldn't figure out what.

"Well, that was a spectacular failure. At least he said he'd go out with me again on a solo date. What was with you tonight?"

"That bastard was going to take advantage of him. You think I was going to let that go?"

"Shug is an adult."

"He was drunk. Just take me home. I'm tired and just want some quiet." I opened the door as he unlocked them, and I dropped into the passenger seat.

I was just tired, and I needed to get up early. I was done with that night.

8

SHUG

"WHAT ARE YOU WEARING?" DREW DEMANDED AS HE STOOD there watching me hanging up a new shipment of leopard print pencil skirts. I'd put one back for myself and then changed my mind.

The question came out of nowhere without even a hello, and I looked down at my black combat boots, jeans, and my white V-neck t-shirt under a plain baby blue dress-shirt. I hadn't even put on makeup that morning. He didn't have to point out I looked like shit. I jerked my gaze up to glare at Drew.

"Hello to you too, Drew. Lovely to see you. How are you today?"

"I'm sorry. I made him go on the date. He didn't even want to. He said you haven't been to see him this week."

"I don't care he went on a date. I have no rights to him. Can we not talk about it?"

When Grey had pulled me in for a hug, those muscular arms holding me to his burly body and the brush of his lips to my cheek, it was like heaven and hell combined. I'd buried my face in his throat for just a minute to inhale the scent of his cologne. It was clean yet spicy, a masculine smell I just wanted to keep drawing into my lungs. His hands wrapped around my sides, and his fingers and thumbs had sunk into my softness. I'd wanted to stand there all night with him. For days I'd tried to convince myself I'd had too much to drink, and my body had taken over. Yet I knew I tried to make myself believe a lie.

"My best friend is a clueless idiot, but no one else is. Don't be mad at him for me pulling the best friend card. My date tried to cancel because his friend came to visit without calling first. I really wanted the date."

I waved off his excuses and moved to the next rack to organize the items again by size. Grey had never looked at me like he had that woman. She was tall, blonde, and built like some fucking supermodel. The jealousy had hit me so suddenly that I was angrier at myself than him. It's not like he saw or felt about me the way I did him. I'd experienced bouts of envy in the past—someone got a partner, a friend married, but I'd never experienced romantic jealousy. The emotion wasn't ingrained in me, and I hated the first experience of that sickening feeling.

"Dammit, Shug, look at me."

"I'm fine. I'm just not feeling well today." That was at least partially true. I felt a cold coming on, and I couldn't afford to be sick. "He's straight. It was good to see him on a date with a woman, just hit me harder than I thought it would."

"You made him lose his cool."

"I didn't make him do anything."

"Oh, telling the man you've had a crush on for years you were hoping for some birthday D with some stranger wasn't a low blow?"

"I'm a grown man. I can fuck whomever I want."

"Dammit, Shug, please, look at you. You're wearing combat boots, for god's sake. A t-shirt. *A. T. Shirt.*"

"I didn't feel well. I didn't want to get dressed up. I didn't commit murder."

"Honey, you haven't dressed up in four days. You've been

in public looking like a frump. You're causing a stir. People are worried about your state of mind. You've skipped lunches with Grey. When is the last time you slept?"

At his question, my hand went to my face, and I stroked the bags under my eyes. I'd let myself go. Part of me thought I'd prepared myself for seeing Grey with a woman one day, but the minute Drew said their dates were there, something in me shut down. I'd drank so much to not remember, but the next morning I'd awakened, and every detail played out in my head.

I'd almost brought home a stranger I didn't even find all that attractive, but I'd wanted to feel a body against mine. Weight bearing me into the mattress. I wanted to not feel empty. Fucking the man mixed with the alcohol, it was something. I'd probably hate myself afterward, but for one night or at least part of it, I'd have a man in my bed.

I'd spent the morning crying like an emotional idiot over a mistake I'd only contemplated making. What would've happened if I'd awakened with some strange man?

"He practically threatened Si to take you home."

"What?"

"When everyone was leaving, he grabbed Si's arm, and I swear he would've caused bodily harm if Si let you get in a vehicle with that guy."

"You're being stupid. You know he's just protective. It's no big deal."

"You're in love with him."

I parted my lips to deny it. To pretend that I felt nothing, but that wasn't the person I was. I'd never learned to mask my emotions or keep things to myself. If I felt someone needed a hug in comfort, I gave it without expectation. If a homeless person asked for change, I gave them what was in my pocket and bought them a meal. My mother had taught me what you give out is what you get back, and to deny something I knew — to lie about it felt unnatural.

"Yeah, but he doesn't feel the same, and I have to be a big

boy and remember that." A lump formed in my throat, and I stopped shifting hangers to kill time and moved behind the counter to start on entering the new inventory numbers I noted on my chart. Next was uploading the images I took to my online store and note what I was putting on the seasonal sale, but I needed the model photos a friend of mine took for me. Those weren't in my email that morning.

I sent the outfits to a photographer friend who did self-portraits of herself in the clothes. She was a size twenty-two and perfect.

Drew jerked the clipboard from my hand, and I looked away from my computer screen. "What?"

"We've all fallen for the straight one before. You're not stupid or whatever else is going through your head. He didn't even like the woman he was with. She kept touching him, and I've never seen Grey mad in all the decades we've known each other. Just don't blame him for me being an asshole. I shouldn't have made him go especially when I knew your party was there. Why didn't you invite him to your party?"

"Carlos said he invited everyone, and I assumed he'd invited Grey. I thought I'd have him to myself like I always do." I roughly ran my fingers through my messy hair making it worse. "When he showed up, he looked so good. And when he hugged—"

"Shug, what's wrong?"

"He just felt right, okay?"

"Then why did you try to go home with that guy then?"

"Because...because I was lonely, and a replacement body was better than no body. I require intimacy and touch; it feeds and grounds me. Even if it's a one-night-stand, at least for a night, I can pretend I'm not alone. But how can I have what I want when the one I do isn't even interested in men?

"I'm lonely, and I don't feel well. I almost made a fool of myself."

"But why have you avoided Grey? You two live for your

shared lunches. He waited for you to show up Monday. Every day that passed…honey, I'm his best friend by default because we've known each other the longest. But you're his best friend now because you spend time together. If I want him to go out, all I have to say is Shug will be there. Don't ruin a friendship with him because of something I forced him to do."

He placed the clipboard on the counter and leaned across it to brush his lips to my cheek. When he straightened, he headed for the door, and I refused to call him back.

I knew I wasn't a prize; I was dramatic and occasionally annoying, but Grey had never once made me feel like I was a bother or found my clothes weird. From the moment he met me, he accepted my gender-nonconformity. Not even a momentary double-take.

He'd been so warm and welcoming; I think a part of me had fallen in love with him the first time I met him. I didn't think a man could get more perfect. Every day we spent together, I learned something that made me like him more. He knew who he was and so settled into a life he loved made him gorgeous to me.

A tickle started in my throat, and I cough so hard I gagged myself. I sat down on the chair behind the counter. I raised my hand to my forehead and tested my temperature. I was clammy and hot. I couldn't afford to be sick. I only had a few part-time people.

I made a mental note to call them to see if they'd work in case I couldn't make it. Rarely did I get sick, but if I did, it was always bad. All I'd need is a few days of rest, and then I'd be good as new, and I'd forget all about how much of an idiot I was. I missed Grey, and it wasn't his fault he didn't want me.

9

GREY

"You let your adorable, little man suffer at home all alone without someone to pamper him?"

Drew's question still played through my mind two hours later as I jogged up the steps of Shug's house. It wasn't odd to go a week without seeing Shug, but after his birthday fiasco, he'd avoided me. For days, I'd wondered what I did. The way he shut down plagued me with something that made me sick to my stomach. After he missed four lunches, I made Drew go by to check on him and he'd said Shug was fine. Something in the way he said it made me believe he lied.

Drew had popped in for lunch, which he rarely did, and the minute he'd mentioned Shug was sick, I'd kicked him out. I'd called in one of my part-time people to close for me, went to the store after a quick trip home to pack a few days' worth of clothes just in case he needed me to stay. I'd already asked someone to run the store for me the next day if something came up. It was a Saturday and usually busy, so I'd needed the second person there.

I raised my hand and knocked hard on the door in case he was in his room at the back of the house. When Shug answered, I barely recognized the normally beautiful man. His eyes were swollen behind his oversized glasses and almost looked as if someone had beat him up. The tip of his pug nose was bright red.

"Shug, why didn't you call me?"

"Do you have a gun in that bag?"

"No, why?"

"If you love me, you'd put me out of my misery." He rubbed at his nose with a wad of balled-up tissues.

He looked so miserable but adorably grumpy at the same time. I stepped over the threshold and wrapped my free hand around the back of his neck. He stumbled a bit when I pulled him into me to press my lips to his forehead. My mom used to do it as a sneaky way of checking my temperature. The heat coming off him worried me.

"Have you been to the doctor?" Without his usual heels on, his head perfectly tucked under my chin.

He sniffled a bit as he leaned into me and his arms twined around my waist. He shook his head.

"Have you taken any medicine?"

"I don't like it."

"Well, I don't care what you like. Into the kitchen, I have stuff for you."

He backed up to glare at me with narrowed eyes. I spun him, and when he didn't start moving, I tapped his ass, and he let out a squeak. He power walked to the kitchen, and I followed closing and locking the door. He stood at the sink, chugging water.

I put all the bags down on the small island, tossed my overnight bag to the floor, and started unpacking the groceries.

"What's all that?"

"I picked up stuff to make you soup. Some juice. Medicine. The pharmacist recommended the best stuff. First, we're going to get some medicine in you. You'll take a shower and get into clean clothes. While you do that, I'll change your sheets."

"I'm not taking the medicine." He squeezed his lips shut and crossed his arms over his chest.

"Baby, if you don't take the medicine, I will hold you down and pinch your nose until you open your mouth. Am I understood?"

"You wouldn't dare."

"Try me." I smirked at him as I tore the safety seal on the cold medicine and removed the plastic dose cup.

He darted his eyes to the only escape exit, he feigned right and then left, and he was on the move. For a sick man, he surprisingly picked up speed as I tried to grab his arm. With the medicine still in my hand, I gave chase. I barely got my foot in the door to bar him slamming it closed, and I listened to him wheezing.

"Fuck, I need to work out more," he muttered as I easily shoved the door open. "Now, Grey, I'm an adult. I don't need the medicine. It makes—"

"And I don't think I asked your thoughts on the medicine."

"Get out." He tried to sound tough, but the pitiful whine in his voice ruined it. The stomping of his barefoot with the pink painted toenails didn't help his cause either.

I made my way into the room, and for every step I took, he countered with one of his own. I positioned myself between the only two ways to get out of the room, the bathroom door would provide him a moment's reprieve, but I could easily pop the lock.

"You want to do this the easy way, baby, or we can do this my way?" I no doubt was about to have a fight on my hands, so I opened the cap and pierced the inner safety seal.

"You're not the boss of me." As soon as the words left his mouth, his eyes widened.

"Is that right, baby?"

"Y-yes."

"You don't sound so sure."

"I-I am." He held up his hands as I advanced. "Now, Grey,

we can be adults here. I'll take the medicine, just leave it on the nightstand."

"You had your chance. We're going to do this my way."

He retreated and hit the foot of the bed; he flailed his arms as he fell. As soon as he landed, he scooted all the way up the bed and covered his mouth with both hands. I climbed onto the mattress and straddled his thighs as he kicked, trying to dislodge me. I snorted at his efforts. I set the medicine and cup on the nightstand and then straightened to stare at him.

I easily removed his hands and secured his wrists above his head with one hand, pushing them into the pillow. "Do I have to tie them down, or will you behave like a good boy?"

"I hate you."

"You can hate me all you want, but you're taking your medicine." My deep chuckle echoed in the room as he rolled his lips between his teeth and sent me a death glare. I poured the proper dose, picked up the cup, and while plotting my demise distracted him, I released his hands and pinched his nose. "You're going to open those pretty lips no matter what I have to do. Who can last longer, baby?"

He was too busy trying to remove my fingers from his nose as his cheeks started puffing out and turning red to realize I had the cup ready. His eyes widened, and then he gasped loudly. As he took a deep breath, I poured the liquid in and slammed my hand over his mouth to make sure he couldn't spit it out.

I placed the cup back on the nightstand and lowered my face to his until our noses almost touched. "I can hold you down all day and you can fight me with everything you have, but you're going to swallow."

He seemed to deflate and lose all his fight. I stared into his big, dark brown eyes, and the second he swallowed, I removed my hand, placed my forearms on either side of his head.

"Better now?" He gave a jerky nod. "Where can I find sheets?" I should be moving, but I enjoyed his softness beneath me. The way he fit against me, and I wondered why I hadn't noticed before how we complemented each other. A thought popped into my head as I realized I'd always put a physical distance between us, and my confusion grew as to why. The minute I knew he was sick; my only thought was to get to him as soon as I could. My brain told me I needed to care for and protect him like I had the other night.

"Hallway closet. Why are you here?"

Did I want to confess that the straight man I was grew confused over the week of being away from him? The longer he avoided me, the more I realized I lived for our lunches. The sightings I had of him. Did I tell him I knew the exact rhythm of the tap of his high heels? Or I could pick his laughter out of a crowded room? Instead of all that, I went with the simplest and safest answer. "Because you're sick, and you need someone to take care of you. I'm not happy I had to find out from Drew." He tried to look away from me, but I trapped his chin in my right hand.

"I don't need anyone to take care of me."

"Yes, you do. You also need a shower. It'll make you feel better. When you're done, come to the kitchen. I picked you up some soup from Ansel until I could make a pot. We can curl up on the couch and watch movies."

"You have to work."

"Klaus and his wife are going to run the store tomorrow for me. I've been thinking of giving Claudine some shifts to get her away from the farm now that the kids are in school full time. I could even give up Saturdays if I let them both work."

Klaus worked for me part-time. Having a farm wasn't always the most profitable business, especially if you had a large family. He came in during the afternoons when his kids got home, and they handled evening chores. I'd give him more hours if I had them to spare. The store was normally a one-person operation.

I couldn't linger on the bed. I eased off him and came to

stand beside it. I watched him as he lay there in rumpled silk pajamas.

"But you love the store."

"I do, but I'm getting older, and maybe taking some time for myself wouldn't be a bad thing."

"Did your date make you think that?" There was a sadness in the question, and I wondered if my date hurt him. It had made me miss his birthday.

"That might be part of it. Could be nice to step out of my comfort zone and find the person for me."

"You should, Grey. You're too nice to stay single. The right woman would love you the way you need."

"We'll see. By the time I get back, I want you in the shower. It isn't healthy to sleep on germ-infested sheets."

He only nodded and sat up. As soon as he threw his legs over the side of the bed, I made my way out of his room. The closet was just beside the guest bathroom, and I opened it to find sheets. Then I grabbed a clean quilt for his bed. I'd wash everything after he fell asleep. With the medicine, I was sure it wouldn't be long.

When I arrived back in his room, his private bathroom door was closed over but ajar. Steam was coming from around the edges, and an image of him naked in the shower filled my head. Shit, I shook it off, but it wouldn't go away. His chest was smooth—I knew that from the way he favored leaving several buttons undone and with him under me, I'd felt the round softness of his belly. My cock jerked, and I tried to ignore it like I'd done since my divorce.

I started stripping the bed and getting it ready for Shug's bedtime.

My brain wouldn't turn off, though. After Brenda left and we'd signed the papers, I'd turned off my needs. Abstinence hadn't been hard because my body wouldn't respond. She always said I was too hairy, too rough, hated the way my hands felt on her skin, and I knew that was only her. The several girlfriends I had in college, except for the excess hair, they hadn't minded being held down—fucked rough.

It would shock everyone to know what the mild-mannered hardware store owner was like behind closed doors. For years I'd pretended I wasn't a sexual person or that I craved to dominate. I left it to jerk off fantasies and nothing more, but once I was single again, I didn't even want those. It was easier to disregard my needs than to open myself to another person who didn't want me.

Holding Shug down, making him submit even about something as little as taking medicine turned me on. Fuck, I should be ashamed of how I'd responded to him. Luckily, my cock hadn't gotten in on it because that would've embarrassed me.

"I thought you'd be done."

I glanced over my shoulder as I was just putting the last pillowcase on to find him standing framed in the doorway. His loose curls were wet and framed his slightly rounded face. He had a towel around his hips, but the thing that I noticed was the tiny barbells through his little nipples. The way the water beaded on his skin and I wanted to lick him—bite him to mark that lightly tanned skin of his.

"Almost done, and get dressed or you'll get a chill. You're already sick enough." I placed the pillow on his bed, and instead of heading for the kitchen like I should've, I crossed the room to him. I pressed my lips to his forehead. "You want a sandwich with your soup?"

"No, I haven't eaten more than crackers the last few days. Probably best not to take the risk."

"Okay, I should have everything ready by the time you get dressed. Put socks on."

Again, I only earned a nod, but the hands that rested on my waist were twisted in my shirt.

"Are you okay?"

"I'm sorry about earlier. I'm not a good sick person. It rarely happens, but when it does, I can get a bit...dramatic."

"Baby, what's different from any other day?" I chuckled as he pushed me, and I backed away to make sure he had food, juice, and to make a nest for him on the couch. I had him all to myself for at least a few days, and hopefully in that time, I could figure out why I wanted the man so damn much.

10

SHUG

THE MINUTE MY EYES OPENED, I FROZE AS THE ROUGHNESS
of stubble on my bare shoulder, and there was a big body
completely curled around mine. None of that made me go into
survival mode. No, that was all because of a thick, hard dick
notched completely between my cheeks. My silk pajama
bottoms and lace thong weren't much protection. My cock
perked up at a deep growl in my ear and strong hips slowly
humped my long-ignored ass.

Last thing I remembered the night before was curling up
on the couch as far from Grey as I could get. My body almost
coiled into a ball after I'd subjected myself to him massaging
my feet and rubbing my lower legs. That combined with a full
belly and the medicine he forced me to take apparently threw
me into a coma.

At the memory of the medicine incident, I grew harder, and
the fact his big, calloused hand rubbed my belly in slow circles
hadn't helped me. When he'd told me I was going to take my
medicine whether I liked it or not, a secret thrill had broken
me out in goosebumps. The way he'd held me down. His voice
gruff and dangerous, tones I'd never heard from him in all the

years I'd known him. I was glad I was so miserable my body hadn't reacted when his weight had pushed me into my mattress.

How many times had I fantasized about Grey doing just that? Would his big hand cover my mouth if I screamed too loudly? Men had told me I was too loud when we had sex. I closed my eyes as I tried to remind myself exactly what his lips felt like on my forehead. Life before was hard enough, but no longer would I have to assume what he felt like holding me or what his dick felt like.

"What are you doing up? It's still early." I slammed my eyes closed as he nipped at my earlobe, tugging on the tunnel I had in the stretched hole.

"Something woke me up."

"Go back to sleep, baby, you need rest."

"Where's my shirt?"

"I took it off you. You were fighting it in your sleep." His casual tone made it seem like we'd awakened together before.

"Um, I normally sleep naked." Why the fuck did I say that?

A growl vibrated my back as his arms squeezed me tighter, and I swore he flexed his hips again. He needed to stop doing that. "I'll remember that for tonight."

"Why are you sleeping with me?"

"Couch was too short, and I wanted to be near you if you needed me. You don't like me in your bed?"

"No, no, it's fine. I'm sure the couch wouldn't have been comfortable for you. It's not really a sleeping couch." It was a vintage couch I'd covered in an indigo velvet. It was more pretty than functional. I clenched my hands in the soft top sheet and heavy quilt as he drew circles on my stomach, dangerously close to my waistband. Goosebumps broke out on my skin. He'd know my cock was hard if he moved any lower.

"Are you feeling better?"

"If I say yes are you going to tell me *I told you so*?"

"No, that's not something I'd do. All I care about is if you're better."

"There's no elephant sitting on my chest."

"Will I have to sit on you to make you take your medicine again?"

"No."

"Shame."

"What?" I didn't know what possessed me, but I rolled to my back to look at his face.

"You're adorably cranky when you're sick."

"I'm so glad you enjoyed treating me like a child."

"I wouldn't have pinched a child's nose, but yours..." He sleepily smiled at me as he squeezed my nose between his middle and index finger. "I really enjoyed that."

"Sadist." I poked his bare, furry chest and ordered myself not to run my fingers through it. It was thick and rough enough to be perfect for grabbing onto when I'd ride him. No, I wasn't thinking about that. Nope, not letting my brain go there.

"Now, now, baby, be nice. If you'd cooperated, I wouldn't have had to do it. You're not going back to sleep, are you?" He shifted and raised up to lean over me, all I'd have to do is lift a few inches, and I could find out what his lips felt like. Were they as firm as I'd imagined or soft?

"No, usually when I wake up, I'm up. This is about the time you get ready for your day. What about your horses?"

"Klaus is going to put them out to pasture for me and check the trough. I'll go back later this afternoon to clean out their stalls and put out feed."

"You look odd all shaggy." I didn't know what came over me, but I lifted my hand to stroke along his rough cheek and jaw.

"I need to trim. Wasn't a priority this week."

"I bet you drove the ladies insane all week with a thicker

beard." I'd said it to remind myself he wasn't mine. There was no realm in which existed I ended up with him.

"Maybe, I don't know. I didn't pay attention."

"Why, Grey? You're sweet if a bit of a closet asshole. You're grounded and know what you want. Doesn't hurt that you're sexy as hell."

"You think so?" His voice dipped into that dangerous register again. The one he'd used right before he'd pounced.

"You don't think you are?"

My embarrassingly sensitive nipples perked up as he drew lazy patterns over my ribs as he seemed to be lost in deep thought.

"I've always considered myself average, passably attractive. I'm built broad. Excessively hairy, something I found some women really aren't into. I'm wired to work like a clock. Me missing Sunday breakfast once caused people to wonder if I was alive or not."

"What do you want? Not what you think is expected, but that one person...woman, what would she be?"

"I want *someone* I guess who wouldn't find my touch distasteful. I've always been an affectionate man. I love touching the person I'm with. Kissing them and not needing a reason to do so. Someone who wants to be loved on but doesn't mind being fucked, too. Someone who wouldn't mind being a little spoiled."

I was about to lose it, and every bit of control I had was being used to stay flat on the mattress. He sounded sad and a bit lonely. He curved his hand around my ribs and stroked upward, and I had to bite the inside of my cheek to keep my moan contained as the rough pad of his thumb brushed my pierced nipple.

"Doesn't sound bad to me. Anyone would be lucky to have you. She's out there, so don't be so quick to give up."

The way he shut down and his eyes went cold shocked me.

He'd never looked at me that way. I was about to ask what was wrong, but he rolled off the bed.

"I'm gonna make coffee. You can get cleaned up, and it'll be done by the time you get there. I'll take the medicine with me just so I can watch you take it." His tone was joking, but his smile was forced.

I'd studied everything about Grey. I knew all his likes and dislikes, or at least I thought I had. He was too even-tempered, and the fact he emotionally shut down worried me. What had I said so wrong that he went from touching me to pulling away? I shouldn't complain about that. His closeness and touch were dangerous to my sanity.

He strode around to my side of the bed and picked up the medicine and the cup, and then exited my room without looking at me again. There I was fighting a hard-on, hairless chest with my man boobs and pierced nipples on display, and I had awakened with the man of my dreams and what had I done: pushed some faceless woman at him to protect myself.

That wasn't me. I was designed to be bold and in your face, but when it came to Grey, he made me so stupid. Yet there was the issue of seeing a new side of him. He'd completely broken his routine for me. Put someone else in charge of the store. Grey had destroyed his comfort zone for me and not to mention that morning. We'd been in bed together, half-naked, and he hadn't moved away when he realized it. I don't remember a time work-roughened hands had ever been that gentle.

Could I ruin five years of friendship with the man I secretly loved?

That's the result that scared me the most. Jenkins wasn't a city; it wasn't like I could avoid Grey if I made a complete fool of myself. None of this was helping. I was sick and vulnerable, and more than a little horny. I'd wait until I was better, and my head was clearer, and I'd made a decision.

I threw the covers off and got out of bed. I went to my

closet to grab my favorite hot pink caftan and went to take a shower. The tightness in my chest was gone. There was no more tickle in my throat, but I didn't want to do a happy dance just yet. I did spend two days in hell not sleeping or eating. One dose of medicine, soup, tea, and a full night's rest, and I felt almost back to normal.

Only if I could get my brain, body, and heart into alignment everything would be perfect, wouldn't it?

11

GREY

THE NEW MYSTERY BOOK I'D BEEN LOOKING FORWARD TO reading lay abandoned on my thigh as I watched Shug sleep. An hour before, I'd saved his e-reader as it had threatened to fall to the floor. The hot pink gown/caftan, whatever he wanted to call it, had a split to expose the length of his thick, smooth legs and some adorable dimples in his thigh. Most of the day, I'd kept our conversations light, normal for us, but the morning still played over in my head.

His lush ass, the way my dick rubbed between those perfect curves. I swore a few more flexes of my hips and I would've lost it, and how fucked up would that have been? After I got him settled on the couch with everything he'd needed, I'd hopped in the shower and taken care of the problem on my own.

I couldn't remember my last orgasm, but I'd clenched my jaw until it hurt to keep from shouting as I shot my load onto the wall. The last time I fucked, I didn't even remember it being that good. The vision in my head had been us in bed— my hips pushed his thighs open as I sank into his tight hole. Kissing him as I twisted my fingers in his soft curls and I could

75

almost feel the drag of his long nails down my back—the biting pain of them.

The ease with which my brain had shifted from feeling off around my friend to wanting to love on him should've shocked me. There was a rightness about it. A sense of peace in the acceptance. He was my complete opposite, and I think that's what I loved the most. He made sure I didn't take myself too seriously.

I just didn't know if he felt the same tension and if so was it was for the same reasons as mine. My hand came up and scratched my bare chest as my free one stroked his soft legs. I wondered if he was naturally smooth or if he waxed since there was no stubble, and his showers were short.

I jerked as his laptop started ringing, and I surged forward to hit the touchpad. I answered the call without thinking, not wanting to wake him up. He still needed his sleep.

"Oh shit, bad time?" A woman filled the screen crossed-legged, wearing an outfit very much like Shug's. Except for the pale skin and blonde hair they favored, her eyes had the same twinkle of mischief his did.

"Shug has a cold, and he's sleeping. I didn't want to wake him. I'm Grey."

"I know who you are. My son finally got smart and jumped you. I'm Star."

"No, ma'am, I found out he was sick, and he needed someone to take care of him."

"Please, as if my blessed child would leave you unmolested when he has you without most of your apparel in his house."

Interesting, I darted a quick glance at my beautiful man.

"Fuck, this is a nightmare." Shug groaned beside me.

"Receiving a call from your life-giver is a nightmare? I'd be insulted if I didn't know you were a brat when you're sick. And this is our weekly call."

"Were you polite, Mom?" He struggled to sit up since he

was still groggy, and I helped him up, smoothing his curls back from his face.

"I'm always polite. What we give out is what we get back."

"Yeah, yeah, positive vibes."

"From what I'm sensing, you won't need another kind of vibe anymore. I'll cancel your late birthday present."

I chuckled as I realized where he got his twisted sense of humor from. "I'm going to go start dinner and let you talk to your mom." I curled my hand around the back of his neck and pulled him in to give him two soft kisses to his temple. "It was nice to meet you. Maybe one day we can do it in person."

"You, too, Grey, and thank you for taking care of him. How did you get him to take medicine?"

"I held him down and pinched his nose until he opened his mouth."

"I'm sure you both enjoyed that."

"Mom, please, have mercy on me."

His mother didn't seem like the merciful type, but I would take pity on him. I got up from the couch and made my way to the kitchen. He was probably sick of soup, so I froze the leftovers and now I needed to find something else to make. His fridge was sorely lacking in anything. I knew he had a habit of shopping daily, and that left us with pretty much nothing except a freezer full of ice cream pints.

"Baby, do you want takeout?" I yelled from the kitchen as I closed the fridge.

"Mom, stop! I'm slamming the lid closed."

I peeked into the living room to find him glaring at his laptop. "Baby, did you hear me?" He went from promising retribution on his mother to gifting me with the same narrowed eyes.

"Takeout is fine. You know what I like."

"I'm sure he does, does he know—"

"Shut up. You have two men. One of them could gag you. Where are my stepfathers? I'll ask them."

I shook my head and unplugged my phone from the charger. I scrolled through my contacts until I found an Italian place Shug liked that delivered. I ordered two of his favorites, along with the dessert he liked, and made my order. They stuttered after I gave the address.

Hoped Shug was ready for this.

I gave them my card information and checked my wallet for cash for a tip. They gave me a total, and I disconnected.

Shug was still whispering to his mom, and his cheeks just seemed to be getting pinker—he was almost red. I was curious about what she said but decided to leave them alone to talk. Making my way down the hallway to his bedroom, I searched in my bag for a shirt and came up with a tank I could wear. It wouldn't lessen the gossip of me being at Shug's in pajama pants on a Saturday night. My truck had been parked in his driveway since last night except for when I ran out to my place for a few hours to take care of chores.

It was probably already spread around town. My phone rang, and I answered without checking the display.

"You're still at Shug's?" Drew's demand hit me as soon as I said hello.

"I left for a bit to take care of the horses, but yes, is that a problem? And how did you know?"

"Well, the diner was abuzz with news of your truck at his place overnight, and I was just in Tony's getting takeout. The owner was talking about you ordering food to be delivered to Shug's. You know what is going to happen."

"Apparently, it's already happened."

"Grey, my mom—oh sorry." He grimaced as he leaned on the doorjamb.

"It's just Drew, baby. What about your mom?"

"Nothing, I was just going to apologize she's—"

"She's the female version of you. It's fine. Dinner will be here soon. I ordered your favorites, so you'd be able to choose."

"Thanks, I'll leave you to talk to Drew."

"I'll be out in a minute. Pick a movie or something." He nodded, and I waited until he was gone. "I already knew the gossip would be flying. I don't care."

"Baby? Really?" Drew's voice went up several octaves.

"Would you like to know he likes to cuddle? Or that he's adorable when he's being bratty? What do you want?"

"Um, Grey, don't fuck with him, okay? There's shit you don't know."

"What don't I know? Is he okay? Seeing someone I don't know about?" I fired off the questions as I started to get angry. I had to stop because I was making a habit of it.

"No, he's just...he's had a thing for you, and you're oblivious. I just don't want you to lead him on. You're like his perfect man."

My man has been keeping some secrets. I really was oblivious. I mean, the flirting was natural, it was just the way he was, and it was too much fun to tease him. I'd gone through a few falling for the straight guy meltdowns with Drew over the years. "I am, good to know."

"Good to know? Grey, please, please, don't do anything hasty."

"When have I ever done anything hasty? I figured something out when he avoided me this week and then taking care of him...I like him. And a man doesn't think about kissing his friends. When he's well, I'm taking him on a date. A real one. Is this going to be a problem between us?"

"Man, we've been friends too long for it to be a problem. Your childhood best friend is bi. Most of your friends are on the LGBT spectrum. Do you need pointers? The best lube? Condoms? Dude, I can totally make a trip to the pharmacy and to his place in fifteen minutes."

"I think I can handle it. And don't make this weird for him. I know you."

"I'm offended. If I knew you'd go for the pretty, femme

boy, I would've started pushing after I realized he was checking out your ass every chance he got." Drew groaned. "Man, I can sense the smirk. When it comes to Shug, it's your go-to with him. Go have dinner, I want details. First kisses are the true proof of attraction."

"Goodnight, and don't be driving by the house. We're going to have enough attention on us as it is."

"The people in this town won't care. They just want you happy, and let me tell you another secret, the rest of this town isn't as oblivious as you are. I think the Fire Chief is still taking bets on when you two will get your shit together."

"Great, now the town thinks I'm clueless on top of being boring."

"Shut up. I still want details, though. I don't think you'll be able to handle him."

All I heard was laughter, and then the call ended. *Asshole.* I tossed my phone on the dresser, dragged my shirt over my head as the doorbell rang. I heard Shug greeting the delivery guy.

"Hold on. I have cash for the tip." I darted into the kitchen and then hurried to the door as I placed my hand on the door and Shug ducked under my arm, running off with the bags. I handed the money over, and a kid I remembered being a regular driver just stood in the doorway. "You okay?"

"Yeah, yeah, um, thanks, night." Before he was off the porch, he had his phone out.

I shook my head as I closed and locked the door. I quickly found Shug doing a little dance as he unpacked the bags.

"My soup wasn't good enough for you?"

"It's food, real food." He moaned, and my cock jerked.

I was going to need to get a handle on my reawakened libido. I walked around the island and pushed up behind him. He stilled and then melted into me, I noticed he tilted his head, and I took advantage, lowered my lips to the side of his neck.

My hands settled on the subtle curve of his hips, and I tugged his ass against me.

"You can't keep doing this to me, Grey. It's unfair." He whimpered as I stroked my hands up to tease his nipples. I'd noticed the way he'd tensed when I'd brushed one that morning.

I drew my lips up to his jaw and back to his ear. My cock was fully invested in getting his fat ass rubbing against it. "What shouldn't I do, baby boy? This?" I pinched and tugged at the bars, his body arched, and I flexed my hips to rub against his ass, showing him that I wasn't playing with him. "Maybe this?" I spun him and lifted him onto the counter, forced my hips between his thighs. I held his jaw in my hands, teased his lower lip with my thumbs as I held our mouths almost close enough to touch.

My heart was beating a pace it had never reached with anyone else. I drew his top lip into my mouth and bit down until he gasped and clutched my sides with his hands. He pulled me deeper into the V of his thighs. His hips arched as his hard dick rutted against mine. Whatever control I possessed was lost the minute I felt the stroke of his tongue.

I was rough and demanding. I took as I palmed his ass and pulled him closer to the edge of the counter, then I was forcing his caftan up until I could feel naked, soft skin. I growled at finding no underwear.

I pulled back to watch his face, he was flushed, and his lips were swollen and parted. His beautiful, long-lashed eyes heavy-lidded as he fought to take a breath.

"We shouldn't do this." I heard the regret clear in his voice. Whether that was from denying our mutual attraction or we might ruin our friendship, I didn't know.

"This is exactly what we should be doing. But before we go any further, I'm taking you on a date. You'll get all pretty for me in those sexy heels you love to tease me with. And when I think you're ready, you're going to end up in my bed. Do you understand me, baby?"

He nodded, and I allowed him one more kiss only because I was selfish.

"I can't believe—" He gasped, and it drew my attention down to find his cock peeking from under the hot pink cloth. I barbell through the swollen head.

I didn't touch him like I wanted. I needed the anticipation —that build-up by all the teasing and waiting that made the coming together so explosive. I took one of his hands in mine and placed it over my dick, let him feel how hard I was. I clenched my back teeth to keep from pushing into his touch. Years of abstinence rode me hard, but I wouldn't ruin this for either of us. I wouldn't regret it. Yet, I had to think about someone other than myself. Sugar needed time to come to terms with the fact I was going to do everything in my ability to make him mine.

"That's all for you. You want it, don't you?"

"Please."

"Not until I say you can. Maybe I'll let you play with your new favorite toy before bed if you're a very good boy." I groaned as his long nails teased my balls, and I pushed into his palm. It took everything in me to remove his touch. Years had passed since anyone other than myself as showed my cock any attention. I dropped a kissed to his mouth as I opened his food, used one of the plastic forks, and started to feed him.

"I can feed myself," he complained even as he opened for me.

"Let me do this, baby boy. I love taking care of you. You want me to pamper and spoil you, don't you?"

"Yes, Daddy."

"Good, baby boy." My cock jerked to remind me I was still turned on, but I was savoring the erection, my second in I don't know how long. Soon, I'd love on him and get off, but I didn't require that. It was the anticipation I needed, and he would submit to me so beautifully when it was time.

12

SHUG

I'D LOCKED MYSELF IN MY BATHROOM, TELLING GREY I WAS going to take a bath since I felt better. The longer I lingered, the more nervous I got. He wasn't going to leave. We'd share a bed again, and I didn't know what the hell I was going to do. I knew what I wanted, what every piece of me demanded, but fear was stealing my sense. My attention went to the mirror, took in my swollen lips and they felt sore from his kisses he made sure he gave me all evening. I was fine if he was touching me, holding me close to his side while we watched whatever movie I chose. I couldn't even remember what it was. Every time he drew circles on my bare thigh, I couldn't help to start shaking.

Without him distracting me, what the hell was I going to do? I'd kissed him. Stroked his thick cock. He'd seen how needy I was. There was no hesitation on his part, and he'd pushed into my touch. He said he wanted to love on me, and those were the words I've dreamed of hearing for years. When he'd pressed his mouth to mine, it had seemed like the most natural thing. What the hell was I going to do if he regretted it? Because my inner cynic started its meltdown. Yet I'd hid it well, or at least I hoped I had.

My biggest fear threatened to become reality. I wasn't feeling sick, and everything I'd ignored hit me. His truck in my driveway for a day and two nights. The delivery boy—I'd seen the shock on his face when Grey came up behind me as I took the food. Hell, I barely tasted dinner. This new Grey had fed me every bite and dessert, too, all while tucked between my shaking thighs.

You can do this, Shug, you're bold, you're confident. No man has ever got the better of you. Call his bluff.

I opened the door in nothing but a towel and found him already in the bed. The sheet and quilt were neatly turned down to the foot of the bed. I swallowed hard and started for my dresser to get a pair of pajama pants.

"We both know you sleep naked. Drop the towel and get into bed." The command in his voice turned me into a damn puddle, and where the hell had that tone come from? It was as if he'd perfected the Daddy voice without trying. That wasn't my quiet and polite friend. I listened to the shifting of his body on the mattress and turned my head.

"What are you doing?" My voice cracked as I found him naked, and he patted the spot beside him.

The corners of his mouth twitched. "Figured if I was naked, you'd be more—"

"Well, it's not helping."

"Come on, baby, get into bed. You need rest. And you might not believe this, but I want to hold you. You know you're safe with me, right?"

I nodded, emotionally he could devastate me, but his physical presence was always comforting and safe. I dropped the towel. I wanted to be brave. For years, I'd searched for the one. What if what I wanted was right there the entire time? Insecurity wasn't normal for me; I'd accepted my body and my personal expression as simply me. I studied his face. The way his gaze caressed me from head to toe and back again and his dick was semi-hard where it rested on his belly. He wasn't ripped—his belly had a bit of a paunch, and he had tiny rolls along his ribs, but his thighs were thick. He was hairy perfection, and I wanted to rub my smooth body all over his.

A squeak escaped me as he smirked and grabbed my hips. He manhandled me until I was sitting astride his muscled thighs.

"I thought you just wanted to hold me."

"I'm holding you, aren't I?" he asked as he looped his arms around my waist. "What's going on in your head, baby boy?"

"That I may have spiked a fever and died."

He chuckled as he gave me a small squeeze. I couldn't remember a time I'd ever felt as free and cherished as when I was with him. It developed before the shift in our relationship. There were always people and places where I didn't feel like an oddity. Humans who just let my irregularities slide into the puzzle with ease. With him, it was simple, too easy, but I loved that I didn't have to contort the parts of me into alignment with him. Yet there was a sliver of fear; I needed the words even though I was terrified they wouldn't be the ones I wanted.

"A part of me says I want this more than anything, and the other is saying we shouldn't. What if you don't want me the way I do you."

"What don't I want, this?" His scruffy cheek caressed mine, and his lips brushed my left cheek. "Or maybe this?" He moved to the other cheek, avoided my mouth, and I pouted. The bastard had the nerve to smirk. "Something about you always drew me in. I didn't think about what that was until you needed me." His warm breath teased my ear and lowered to the side of my neck.

A whimper escaped as he sucked at the sensitive spot just under my ear. My back arched as his rough palm and fingers stroked over my belly, chest, caught on my nipple piercing and then he was curling his hand around the back of my neck. As he started to retreat, I hugged his neck to keep him close. I feared that if he broke contact that the spell would lift, and he'd rethink holding me.

"Be calm. I'm not going a place, baby. This may seem quick, but there is nowhere in the world I would rather be."

The sincerity in his husky voice and his eyes, which locked onto mine as he'd spoken, eased the tension. My reward was his smile and his gaze dropping to my lips.

"Let me show you how well I can take care of you. All I want is a chance, slow or fast. This is all at your pace. I know what I need. I just have to wait for you to catch up."

As I opened my mouth to answer, his lips met mine. He kissed me soft and sweetly, as if it was a promise of more. His fingertips pushed into my flesh as he pulled me into him. We were naked in my bed. Nothing to bar him or I from taking this to naughtier places, but I savored the gentleness and laziness. As I scored his scalp with my nails, a groan rumbled his chest against mine.

He retreated and advanced between kisses as if he couldn't bear for us to be separated. His dick was hard where it aligned with mine, and our breathing turned ragged as we moved in a seamless dance.

"God, baby boy, you feel so fucking good." His fingers moved to the back of my head and gripped my hair, pulled my head back. He licked and sucked down the front of my neck. The nip and pressure intensified as he reached my chest. My thighs shook and tensed against his sides as he tugged at the barbells.

My hips involuntarily moved, rutting against the crisp hair on his lower belly. He was so warm and solid, smooth skin and hair, he was rightness came to life.

"You're Daddy's good boy, aren't you? Want to make me happy?" he asked as he released my hair, and I lowered my head to meet his heavy gaze. His cheeks were ruddy, and his lips swollen from our kisses.

"Yes." I brushed my mouth to his as I tried to catch my breath.

I didn't want to be in control here. I needed to be loved and used. Touch and sex were something I required to be connected to a person on a level where they cherished my neediness. Fed that hidden part of me until I felt whole.

A small, yet sharp smack to my right ass cheek brought me back to myself, physically ordered me to focus. "Yes, what?"

"Yes, Daddy."

"That's right. When we're together, you'll allow me to spoil and pamper you. Show you in every way who you belong to. Show you how beautiful I find you when you're simply yourself."

He kissed me between words. I whimpered as his touch turned rougher, molding the parts of me people had found distasteful in the past to fit just his hands. He turned us so he rested his hips between my thighs. His weight sinking his angles into my softness. He curved his left hand around the back of my knee and drew it upward. I arched my back, and my head pushed down into the pillow as all my anxieties faded.

"I'm going to love on you all night. Worship every curve and dip. So responsive. I love that sharp little gasp when I kiss you right here." His teeth tenderly sank into the spot behind my ear. "Oh, yeah, that one. Or the way you arch when I play with your nipples." He latched onto one of them, and just as he knew I would, I arched. "Oh, fuck, that needy little whine is enough to get me off."

"Grey, please."

"No, baby boy, we're not rushing. We have all the time in the world. Just let me love on you. This isn't about us getting off. This is us finding pleasure in each other. No time limits, no rush to an end. Just you and me, and what we feel. So, baby, just feel."

Submitting was the easiest and hardest decision I'd ever made.

"Do you trust me?"

He brushed kisses to one cheek and then the other, pulling back until his gaze locked on mine. His smile serene, the corners of his eyes crinkled with happiness. At that moment, he was everything and I couldn't deny him.

"Yes, Daddy."

"Good boy."

13

GREY

THE PAST FEW DAYS HAD BEEN SOME OF THE BEST I remembered. As much as I attempted to rein myself in, I couldn't. Sunday, we'd awakened, kisses and cuddling. I'd missed breakfast at the diner again, but I hadn't cared people would know where I was that time. My boy enjoyed being touched and held, seemed to have an uncontrollable impulse to run his fingers through the thick hair on my chest. We'd learned more about each other, he told me more about his life growing up, his mom and dad, who he didn't have a close father/son relationship with, but they were friends. I learned about numerous stepfathers and stepmothers, his chosen family and friends. His mother being Poly had made me a little unsure, but he made a point of saying that her choice wasn't his. He was happy to find one man. I had to admit I wasn't a sharer when it came to him.

I told him about Brenda and her four-year relationship with someone on a neighboring ranch. His shock at her wanting someone other than me soothed a hidden part of my ego and pride that had taken a major hit. I couldn't remember a time where I'd just laid in bed with someone to have a lazy morning. When it was time to take care of the horses, he'd gone with me. Touching him was turning into an addiction. We'd made the trip to my place with my fingers tucked between his soft, thick thighs.

We'd made out, touched each other until we were on the edge of release, but every time I'd gently brought us back only to start again. He'd begged me to get him off, but I refused. I'd touched every inch of his beautiful body with my fingers and lips. I'd sucked him, enjoyed the textures, the silkiness of his dick, and the hardness of his piercing. I'd thought having a cock in my mouth for the first time would feel strange, but it was Shug, and his pleasure turned me on. I hadn't allowed him to return the favor; he'd seemed shocked I didn't demand him to suck me off.

His responsiveness tested the strength of my patience. After a night of playing with him and holding him, I knew every spot that made him moan or gasp. He had a dozen different sounds, a specific whimper when I brushed the spot just behind his ear or nipped his hard nipples, tugging at the tiny bars. I'd memorized every one of them and I was dying to hear them again, but I needed him to know I wanted him for more than a quick fuck. After our weekend, I was sure he was the one I'd waited for, and I wasn't going to give him up.

I'd awakened every morning hard from dreams of my boy's lips wrapped around my cock. The way he'd eventually greedily take whatever I gave him. My dominance turned him on, and I couldn't wait until the time we could explore how much I could tease him until he begged me to fuck his beautiful, soft ass. I'd put the sexual side of myself away for so long that the arousal was overtaking my typical caution. As I dealt with the frustration, I also savored the low hum of restlessness which became normal, and I wanted more of that.

After I'd touched him, accepted what he was to me, I realized what that odd emotion riding me whenever I was around or thought of him was. I'd gone so long without finding anyone attractive I'd forgotten. I'd wanted him for far longer than the last few months. The person I wanted being a man didn't bother me; it didn't make me question myself. My need for him just was. As natural as any attraction I'd had in the past. Yet, he was different in one big way. I could see myself growing closer to him, building a life with him. That revelation was too soon to confess. Soon I'd tell him, but until then, I'd show him just how much I valued him.

I adjusted myself as I finished getting ready for our first date. I'd made reservations at The Orchard; it was the nicest place in town, and the menu had a lot of Shug's favorites. We hadn't seen much of each other over the week as he caught up at the store from him being sick, although we'd shared lunch a few times. I'd behaved as much as possible to make sure I didn't overwhelm him. I knew he was still a bit unsure of what happened between us.

If I was honest, as sure as I was about my feelings for him, due to my habit to question most things, I'd waited for an awkwardness to descend over my happiness. That hadn't happened, though. So, I was bisexual, or I was just attracted to the person he was. I thought he was perfect, and I was going to make sure he knew how I felt. We'd gone further than I'd planned.

Our date was about us spending time and learning about each other as a potential couple, but it was also to show I wasn't ashamed of him. I slipped on my peacoat, put my phone and wallet into the inside pocket, grabbed keys, and made my way downstairs. Closing up the house, I jogged to my truck, impatient to get back to him.

I was nervous about wearing out my welcome. I'd suppressed my affectionate nature to the point I was scared he'd become sick of me. Being the person I'd hidden with him was important to me; I didn't want to pretend to be something I wasn't to keep him.

It seemed to take forever to pass the town limit sign, and then I was pulling up in front of his house. I parked and exited

my truck; I made my way up the walkway and knocked on the
door. A few minutes later, I heard the deadbolt click, and the
door was opening. My mouth curved into a smile and then it
fell as I took in my beautiful man.

He was wearing a pink tuxedo shirt with the ruffles, much
like the one he wore the night of his birthday. He had a black
pencil skirt, striped tights, and his high-heeled ankle boots.

"You look beautiful. I'm feeling underdressed." I stepped
over the threshold, and he countered until I could close the
door.

"You're perfect."

He nibbled on his gloss-covered lower lip. I snagged him
with my arm around his waist and tugged him to me. He
melted into me, giving me his weight.

"If I wasn't such a gentleman, I'd suggest staying in and
getting takeout."

"We don't have to —"

I used my left hand to lift his gaze to mine that had fallen to
my chest. "I'm taking my boy out to dinner. Show off how
lucky I am." I brushed my lips to his and felt his shy, little
smile. "Sugar, I'm not ever going to hide you. I know you're
nervous about this, but I'm not ashamed about being attracted
to you. And if I'm honest, I've felt this way for a long time. I
just didn't recognize it. It's been so long since I've wanted
anyone."

"And I've always been attracted to you, from the minute I
walked into the store that first morning."

"You were wearing red stilettos, a black sheath dress, and a
red trench coat. You kept pushing your thick-framed cat-
eyeglasses up your nose."

"You remember what I was wearing? Was it because I was
weird?"

"No, it was because of how confident you were and how
beautiful. You walked in with your head held high, and I
instantly liked you because you were just you."

"Find glasses sexy, huh?"

"Definitely on you."

"Maybe I'll wear them more for you."

"Whatever you want. Are you ready for our first date?"

"Yes. Where are we going?"

"The Orchard. I made reservations for us. I thought about taking you somewhere fancier, but I never want you to think I'm hiding you."

"Not much chance of doing that in Jenkins." He chuckled as I helped him on with his coat, and he put his phone and wallet in his pocket.

"Getting sick of small-town life, baby boy?" I asked as he walked out onto the porch and I locked and closed the door behind us.

"No. Part of me thought maybe the newness would wear off, and my lack of anonymity would be too much, but it never happened."

"Good. I kinda like you, and long-distance wouldn't work for me."

He rolled his eyes, and I rushed forward to open the door for him. I easily helped him into the truck and buckled him in, taking the opportunity to brush my lips to his again.

"You're going to be wearing more gloss than I am by the time we get to The Orchard."

"Not a problem, but I'm sure it looks way better on you than me."

I closed the door and went around to the driver's side. Again, I wanted this date to be perfect for him. I knew his dating experience since moving here disappointed him. I knew he'd be happy with a movie and takeout or sitting on my store counter sharing lunch as a date. He needed to learn that I was proud to be with him. We had plenty of time for cozy nights in on the couch or in bed, but not for our first official date.

The trip to the restaurant didn't take but ten minutes, and

as I parked, I told him to stay until I came around to open his door. I started to pull the handle to get out, but I hesitated.

"Before we really get going on this date, does it bother you that I want to open a door or pull out your chair? I was taught to be a gentleman with my dates."

"You've always done it. Why stop now? You won't change what's natural for me, and I'll return the favor. To be honest, you being all gentlemanly and sweet is a bit of a turn-on."

"I just don't want to make you uncomfortable. That's important to me."

"We're fine. Now, open my door. I'm hungry."

"How close to hangry are you?"

"You don't want to know." He grinned, and I rushed to get him inside.

I kept my arm around his waist as we made it across the parking lot, and once we stepped inside, everything went quiet. The place was packed.

"Are they paying for dinner and a show?" he whispered, and I spread my hand across his lower back as I told the grinning hostess I had a reservation.

The whole damn town probably knew. Please, don't let this ruin the night for him.

"I'm sorry."

"Grey, don't apologize. If you're not bothered, I'm not. We had to know they'd be curious."

"I know, but—"

"Grey, we're fine, hangry, remember?"

"Shit, okay."

We were shown to our table, and I pulled out his chair, then took mine.

"Your usual drinks?"

"Iced tea for me. Baby, you want your martini or something else?"

"Iced tea."

"That's two, thanks."

"Your server will be right here with your drinks."

I waited until she was gone. "You can have a drink."

"I know I can. Don't worry so much."

"You know who you're talking to, right?"

He leaned forward, his hand sliding over the tablecloth until I laced my fingers with his. "You want tonight to be perfect, and I appreciate that, but this isn't just my first date but ours. I want you to relax, just be with me, and we'll be good. I never asked why you didn't drink. Some people have reasons, and others just don't like it."

"I think I did enough drinking and other things in my college days to last me a lifetime. There was never alcohol in the house when I was growing up. I had the occasional beer in the pasture parties back in high school, but at college, I went a little overboard with my freedom. I nearly flunked out of college my sophomore year. The college binge drinking took its toll on me."

"I can't imagine that."

"What about you, party in college?" I was determined to ignore everyone who watched us. Pretended no one else existed but him.

"I was the social Queen Bee. I loved it, but I'd been smoking and drinking since the start of my teens. My mother isn't the strict type."

"Doesn't seem to be." I stroked my thumb along his and his full lips lifted into the smile I'd always loved.

"After college, I became a proper adult and kept my partying for the weekends or nights where I didn't work the next day. I was never one for expectations or rules. I got older and there were bills to pay, goals I wanted to accomplish, and the partying just died down."

Jenny, a server I recognized, dropped off our drinks. "Y'all ready to order, or you need a few more minutes?"

"A few more minutes, Jenny, thanks." I lowered my voice. "Are they waiting to see if this is an official date or what?" I winked at Shug's adorable eye roll.

She leaned down to whisper. "The fire chief has the betting sheet, but I think they're a few pools. Like a first official date, there's even one when and if you get married. Tonight, is about the official date, or if they're starting from the takeout at Shug's place. I'm sure there will be a rush on the others after confirmation."

Shug snorted and almost choked on his tea. "This town needs better entertainment than us."

"Shug, they've been running this game since you two shared your first lunch. The stakes are high," Jenny said with a giggle.

"What should we do, Grey, make someone wealthy or make them wait?"

"It's an official date," I answered loud enough for everyone to hear, and there was a loud whoop from a table near the bar.

"Pay up. Mama needs bingo money." Old Lady McIntyre rushed to the Chief's table to collect her winnings.

People started filing out, grumbling to themselves, and I met Shug's gaze across the table.

"Thanks."

"What are you thanking me for, baby?"

"I didn't want this to be hard on you. You grew up in this town and—" His voice broke slightly, and he dropped his chin to his chest.

I stood up and went around the table, knelt beside his chair. I placed my fingertips under his chin to turn his face toward me and stroked my thumb along his lower lip. "I am not ashamed. Yes, I grew up here. Yes, I was married to a woman. Yes, I stayed single for a long time. In no way does your gender affect how I feel about you or the possibilities that we have. You changed everything the minute you walked into my store; I just didn't realize it until recently. We're going to have our first date. Second date. First fight and hundredth fight. We're going to be a normal boring couple one day, and I'm looking forward to that."

"Okay, sorry. It's just the town…you're like a pillar of the community. A constant, and I didn't want how the town viewed you to change."

"They'll view me how they want. If they have issues with me being with you, then that's on them. I'm not giving up the chance. I waited a very long time for you." I leaned in and brushed my lips to his. "We're going to have dinner and conversation, and then I'll drive you home, kiss you at the door all gentlemanly, and if I'm lucky, I'll get to cuddle you while you sleep."

His cheeks turned pink, and I loved the shyness of the normally bold man. I stood and looked around to find everyone watching and smiling. They could think what they wanted, but just as I'd told him, I wasn't ashamed.

14

SHUG

"CAN I STAY WITH YOU TONIGHT? I MISSED HOLDING YOU IN MY sleep."

Those words still played in my head as I got ready for bed. The date he'd set up was perfect. Admitting to myself at least that I'd carried a bit of fear about what it would be like to take our budding relationship public. Us together didn't send my life into a cataclysmic shift. I was still out and proud, but for him, it changed how the town and everyone who knew him viewed the man who grew up there. I shouldn't have worried. He'd soothed me the entire time, as sweet as he'd always acted with me. The only big change was his affection, and I was loving that, too.

He'd told me to take a bath and relax, that he'd lock up and set the coffee for the next morning. I'd forgone the soak, but I'd taken a hot shower and relaxed. Coming out of my bathroom, I nearly swallowed my tongue at finding a perfectly formed man in my bed. Several inches of beautiful dick making my damn mouth water. How long had it been since I had a cock like that choking me?

"Grey?"

"Baby boy, you're safe. You're always safe with me. I'll

keep telling you as many times as you need me to. If all you want is to sleep, that's what we'll do, but I'd prefer if you'd let me love on you a little like the other night. That's your choice. If you don't fully trust this yet, that's fine. It's a huge step to go from friends to lovers."

There was the Grey I knew, the caring one, the one who wanted to make everything okay for me. Did I want to fuck up my chance just because losing him terrified me? I removed my towel and draped it over the empty laundry hamper beside my dresser.

I made my way slowly toward the end of the bed and bent over, my hands sinking into the mattress and then my knees joined them. I focused on his smile as he sat all the way up and patted his thighs. The coarse hair on his legs teased my smoother ones until I seated myself straddling his lap. I whimpered at the feel of muscled thighs under my ass, and his cock lined up with mine.

"Fuck, you're beautiful and sexy. How did I get so lucky?" His voice was deep and filled with need as he placed his hands on my knees, stroking upward and I had no choice but to arch into the press of his fingers and palms. "So soft. So perfect."

I was trembling so badly, and my breathing was nothing more than shuddered inhales and exhales. His left arm curled around my lower back and tugged me until I was even closer, my thighs wider.

"Is-is this weird for you?" I had to ask. It didn't matter that we'd made out and he'd tortured me with extended foreplay, even sucked my dick like a natural, but we hadn't discussed our physical relationship going beyond where it already was.

"Why, because you're a man? No, because you're Shug. If I'd known how you belonged in my bed, you'd have been there sooner." His nose nudged my chin until my head fell back and the hard tip of his tongue drew down the front of my throat. He stopped to nip and suck, and I clutched at his head as he reached my nipples. He wasn't afraid to use teeth, and I wanted more—harder. "Can you forgive me for being clueless?"

"You were straight."

"No excuse. I should've noticed how much I loved you in those heels of yours. The way I waited for the sound of your voice when you came for lunch. How much I lived for your smile."

My hips shot backward as fingertips stroked over my hole, massaged around it and giving me only the barest pressure. How long had it been since someone other than myself had played with my ass? He'd teased my ass but only with the softest touch, never with the intention of entering me.

"I'm gonna tear that tight little hole up one day soon."

"Not tonight?" I asked as I pushed down slightly and felt the pop of the tip of one finger.

"You're gonna be a slutty boy, aren't you?"

"I'm whatever—" I gasped as he rubbed around inside my rim. So long since I'd felt anything other than my toys. "Daddy wants me to be."

As soon as it was out, all control he had was gone, and I was easily flipped onto my back. His mouth slammed down on mine as his bulk forced my thighs wider. His balls slapping my ass as he rutted our cocks between our bellies. I tasted his growl as I dug my nails into his back, and the harder I scratched him, the harsher he kissed me.

"I want to suck you, Daddy." I'd beg; I'd do whatever he wanted me to do. I almost cried as he lifted his weight from me, fearing I said something wrong, but then I was terrified when he placed his hands on the backs of my thighs and forced my knees towards my shoulders and he looked down.

"I did promise the other night you could play with your new toy if you were a good boy. Is that what you want?"

"Please."

Every part of me ached. I felt empty, but as much as I wanted to get off. Having him show me what being loved on by him would mean—the last time we'd shared a bed he'd played me perfectly. Forced me to the edge and drew me back. We'd both gone to sleep hard and needy, but it was the connection—the tease that made it so intense. He made it seem like loving on me was enough to make him happy. The end—the release—wasn't the goal, but the pleasure we took in the whole act.

He backed up as he stroked his cock, the pre-cum beading in the slit. "I want you on your hands and knees facing me."

He didn't have to tell me twice as I did what he asked, and the head brushed my lips as I waited for permission. The first smack of his hand on my ass cheeks, one then the other, had me screaming. He thrust his hips forward, the swiftness of it choked me, and I instantly relaxed as I let him fuck my mouth, swallowing around the tip when he sank into my throat.

"Fuck, boy." His hands shook as he stroked them up and down my back. I opened wide as I let him use me, his upper body curled forward, and my hips lifted to let him tease my hole. I loved his balls slapping against my chin. The way he growled what a good Daddy's boy I was. I could come with him just fucking my throat and fingering me. I braced my hands as he suddenly grabbed my hair and forced my face into his groin until his pubes tickled my nose. He froze there for a minute before he jerked away, and he made me get to my knees.

His big hands circled our dicks and jacked them in a brutal rhythm as he kissed me, my slutty whines muffled, but the louder I got, the harder he squeezed our lengths.

"You almost made Daddy come too quick, but that needy little throat wanted Daddy's load." His rough words were spoken against my lips as I grabbed handfuls of his chest hair.

I nodded, but he didn't need me to say yes or no; he knew. I bit down on my lip as I felt the tension building.

"Don't you fucking dare be quiet. You let me hear it. I want everyone to hear how much you need me."

The sting of my scalp as he pulled brutally at my hair had me racing toward my release. The bite of his teeth into my lower lip fed my lust. The dirty talk and the uncontrolled stroking of our cocks and I let out all the noises no one ever wanted to hear from me. Every whimper and plea, every screamed *Daddy* that tore at my throat, and then I was clutching his around his neck as I shot onto our bellies, and seconds later, I heard his shout as his joined mine. His cum covered hands stroked up my belly, squeezing the curve of it as if he really did love my curves.

The feral kisses of moments earlier had shifted to softer ones. Words of praise slipping from his mouth as he held me to his chest. Both of us breathing roughly as we slowly started to calm.

"Are you okay, baby boy?"

Was I okay? And there was only one answer. "Yeah."

"We need to take a shower and get you tucked into bed."

"Are you staying?"

"Where else would I want to be?"

And he made it sound so simple. His entire life changed when he stepped outside my door and into the real world for our first date, but he made it so natural. He couldn't stop kissing me, every time he'd pull away, he was back, and I squeaked as he lifted me from the bed. I wrapped my legs around his waist. He easily carried me to the bathroom to take a shower.

It was all too easy, wasn't it? All the failed relationships and one-night stands, how could it be so easy to fall for a man you considered your best friend? Someone who you believed was completely off-limits became the one.

He started the shower with one hand as I held onto his solid body with my arms and legs. He grinned as he kissed me, whispered praise that I never dreamed I needed until him. So many of my needs were ignored, and it was overwhelming to be cared for by him. It was too perfect, but I wouldn't ruin this. I wasn't going to question. He was mine and I was his, and that's all that mattered.

"Drop your legs, baby boy. I'll get us cleaned up and tuck you into bed. We'll go to the diner for breakfast. Pancakes piled with strawberries and whipped cream, right?"

I loosened my legs and dropped my feet to the floor, and I stood in front of him. "How do you know so much about my likes and dislikes?"

"When you care for your person, you remember things. It's the small things, Sugar. Lives together aren't built on grand gestures. It's the way they take their coffee. Their favorite sweater brought to them on a chilly night. It's remembering what's important to them. I can't buy you the world, but I can give you good memories that will make you smile when you think of me. We're still new...still learning, but we have time to be us. That's all I want."

If I hadn't fallen for him a long time ago, that answer would've sealed it for me. I hated that women in the past made him feel less than for doing what made him happy. He was everything I needed and never knew it. And it was more than how handsome and sexy I found him. He possessed a sweetness and a compassion a lot of men rejected. He embraced the caring and commitment I'd searched for on countless dates.

"I want that, too."

"Good, now let's shower and I can get back to cuddling you. I swear my bed is lonely when I'm not with you."

Emotion locked the words in my throat. He made everything right. He did so much right, and I was going to trust in myself and him. He'd never given me a reason not to. He made it sound like forever, and, god, I wanted that so much.

15

GREY

A MONTH HAD PASSED SINCE OUR FIRST DATE, AND THERE weren't many nights we spent apart. Sometimes I forced myself to drive him home or go to my place after our shared evenings. We grew closer every day, but I still worked not to overwhelm him. Saturdays were our date nights. Every week he chose something he wanted to do. That night he wanted to stay curled up on the couch with me, and I wasn't complaining. I loved having him all to myself, no matter what we did.

I bent down the edge of my newspaper to find Shug scrolling through his phone. His oversized glasses perched on the end of his adorable nose. He was seated on the opposite end of the couch between my legs with his rested over mine. His brows drawn together. For a few weeks, I'd noticed he'd had something on his mind. I knew the holiday season was coming up and work got busier, especially online orders.

"What's with the worry lines?"

"Why do you think I'm worried?" he asked without looking up from the screen.

"Not playing that with me, baby boy." I slowly folded my paper and laid it on the coffee table. I patted my thighs. "Put your phone aside and sit right here." I patted my lap, and I waited for some argument, but he did exactly what I asked.

Removing his glasses, he placed them and his phone on top of my newspaper. He moved to his knees and crawled across the cushions to settle across my thighs. I wrapped him in my arms. He laid his head on my shoulder. I kissed his forehead. He so easily let me take care of him, and I loved it.Aand while I let him get away with some things, if something bothered him, I needed to know what that was.

"So, tell me what's wrong? You're a strong, independent person, but if there's something I can help with, I need to know."

"I know, I really do. Halloween is coming up."

"I can't wait to see what your costume is gonna be. Last year's left very little skin to the imagination. This year I'm going to enjoy the flashing a lot more knowing I can touch you." He giggled as I slipped my hand under the hem of my t-shirt he wore. I didn't understand this possessiveness at seeing him in my clothes. It had never been that way in the past, not even with Brenda at the beginning of our marriage when we still believed we were happy.

"Those worked for you, Daddy?"

"They did pique my curiosity, just a bit."

"I'll have to come up with something even better this year."

I knew what he was doing, and he wouldn't distract me. "That didn't answer my question, though. Why's Halloween got you so quiet? My baby isn't the quiet type." I suppressed my chuckle at his bratty heavy sigh.

"It's not really about that. I usually go to my mom's place for Thanksgiving and Christmas. Mom wants to bring my step-dads here for the holidays...to meet you."

"Okay, is there a reason that makes you nervous? You can go there if you're not ready, but I have talked with your mom before, even since we started dating." I manhandled him until I got him astride my thighs so he couldn't hide his expression from me. "Look at me when you answer. Just be honest, if you're not ready, then I'll respect that."

He lifted his arms to rest them on my shoulders and linked his hands behind my neck. "It's not that, I promise. But those were calls or video chats. This is in real life, can't just pretend to lose wi-fi or a call *mysteriously* drops."

"Are you upset about what I'll think of your parents?"

"A little. I'm not embarrassed about my family or friends. I love them. It's how I grew up. We don't understand boundaries or sometimes clothes."

"I already know your mom and stepfathers are nudists and very laid-back people. That doesn't make them bad. I want to meet your parents, even your dad, one day. Family isn't something I've had in a long time, and I'd very much like to share yours but only when you're ready. This is your choice, and I'll support whatever that is."

"So, you'd deal with my craziness—"

"Baby boy, I already deal with your craziness, have for—" He growled at me, and it was adorable. "I adore you, and eventually, I'll meet them in person, whether that's this year or next."

"Can I stay here while they crash at my house, and then you can help me disinfect my bed?"

His impish grin shocked a laugh out of me. "I'll buy you a new mattress. To answer your question, any excuse to have you close, I'll take it."

"Why are you so sweet?"

"I've been told I'm suffocatingly over-affectionate."

"You're perfect. I like that you're caring and sweet. I love that you stop by my house in the morning if I don't spend the night just to kiss me before work. The goodnight calls. I've known you for several years before this developed, I liked everything before, and I like it even more now. Are you worried that you'll do too much?"

"I do. I worry that I'll hover too much. That my gentlemanly ways will get to be annoying. That my compulsion to touch and, on occasion, be a bit dominant will tire you out. Or that my need for quiet time or my lack of desire to party will finally bore you."

"I'm not her or any other woman that you've known in the past. You need to be yourself with me. You respect me for being myself. Why wouldn't I show you the same? So please, Grey, just be you."

"I will. I'm sorry. We're new in many ways, but I guess I forget you've known me for five years."

"You don't have to apologize." He leaned in and rested his forehead on mine.

I cupped his jaw and brought his head forward until our lips touched. "Promise me if something worries or bothers you that you'll always come to me. When I told you you're safe with me, I meant it."

"Your *Daddy* voice is really, really nice. I always thought so."

I chuckled as he cuddled close to me. "Did I use it before? I just thought it was my voice."

"It is. You just have this quiet confidence. This strong way you carry yourself. I've always felt so comfortable and safe with you from the minute I met you. You don't know how many times I jerked off, imagining that voice in my head. I was always scared that you'd notice."

"If you didn't notice, I was oblivious, baby boy. I was just being me, and yes, I felt a bit odd around you." I caught his frown. "Not in a bad way. Then the night of the infamous date, I kept an eye on you, and when you left, I threatened Si to make sure you made it to bed...alone." I took a deep breath. "Then Ansel mentioned the cousin, and it suddenly hit me that I shouldn't feel jealous. I started questioning myself, my intentions, and then you got sick. The happiness I experienced when I was around you. The way I craved our conversations and lunches. After I accepted it for what it was, it was natural.

Even if it had caused some people in this town to turn their backs on me, you're worth whatever they could throw at me. Yet we didn't have issues. Apparently, most people knew how clueless I was."

"I wasn't any better. You should've been inside my head the night of Carlos's party when I mussed you. I didn't want anyone looking at you. If Drew hadn't sat on my lap, I would've fixed you."

"Possessive, huh?"

"You know it, Daddy, I already told you I'm too much of a diva to share."

"I don't share either. So, we're good about your mom and stepdads coming for the holidays. We can make dinner here, you can stay with me in my bed where you belong, and they can go to your place."

"We're good. I didn't mean to worry. It's just my family is odd, and you won't have a minute of quiet or privacy while they're in your house. I don't want you to be overwhelmed or think you must like them. If it gets to be too much, all you have to do is tell me and go have some quiet time. Go for a ride. I need us to always be honest with each other. If you need space from me, it's yours."

"Same for you."

I nodded and brushed his lips with mine, hugging him to my chest and savoring the softness and warmth of his body. Holding him put me at peace. Taking care of him made me feel whole. How I hadn't realized it sooner, I didn't know, but I reminded myself that the time may not have been right.

"What do you want for dinner, baby boy?"

"Whatever you want to make, Daddy. I'm hungry."

"You want to keep me company?"

"You know I love to watch you cook."

As I lurched forward, he squeaked, and I threw my feet to the floor. I easily carried my boy to the kitchen and seated him on the counter, kissing him before I went to see what I had to cook for dinner. All I ever wanted was someone to care for, to be happy, and I was finally there. I'd lived with insecurity for so long that it hadn't disappeared as I'd liked. I'd give it time; he had no complaints about me. I'd enjoy my time with him and leave all the bullshit from my past where it belonged. He was mine, and that's all I cared about. Everything else would work itself out.

16

SHUG

I parked my car beside Grey's truck and cut the engine. The party was a bust, not because it wasn't fun but because Daddy wasn't there to appreciate my costume. I leaned into the back seat and pulled out the hat with dyed black feathers and sequins; I'd spent a week making it. Putting it on, I secured the strap under my chin. I held my black trench coat closed as I made my way to the porch and ascended the steps.

The door was unlocked, and I let myself in and called Grey's name. He appeared from the living room; he tipped his head from one side to the other. He took in every inch of me, and as he stared, I untied the sash around my waist, removed it, and let it drop to the hardwood floor.

"You did not go to Shane's in stiletto boots, thong, harness, and black feathered headpiece."

I stood there in my thigh-high boots, looking like a goth Carnival attendee and grinned at my Daddy. He wore nothing but a pair of jeans, his hairy chest on display. I still couldn't believe that man was mine—my Daddy. He wore a stern expression, but I didn't miss the heat in his beautiful eyes. I leaned back against the door and heard the lock click. My headpiece tipped by the weight of it, and I caught it before it fell. He didn't want to go to the bar for the costume party, and I told him I'd only go for a few hours and then come home to his place.

I'd lasted an hour; it hadn't felt right being there without him. Everyone had asked where my man was. I appreciated he told me to go, that it wouldn't bother him. He didn't want to change me, and I wouldn't change him for the world. I had my nights out with my friends for a few drinks here and there. We both agreed he wouldn't enjoy his time at the bar but didn't want me to turn down hanging out with my friends.

"Don't like it, Daddy?" I drew my bottom lip between my teeth.

He lifted his left arm and then twirled his index finger in a circle. "Give me a turn." His tone went from husky baritone to a dangerous growl, and a shiver shimmied up and down my spine.

I grinned as I strolled toward him a few feet to spin on the pointed toes of my boots and only made it half-turn before I whimpered as he pressed to my back. I dropped my head back onto his shoulder, and I arched my hips backward as he cupped my bare ass cheeks in his big rough hands.

"You show all those horny men what belongs to Daddy?"

"But it's only for Daddy to touch."

"That's not what I asked."

"Yes, Daddy."

"Take off the headpiece." He growled in my ear, and I didn't hesitate to obey as I undid the strap under my chin. As I removed it, he lowered his mouth to my shoulder and bit down —pain and pleasure made me tense. I dropped it to the floor and reached back to grab his thighs, and my pointed nails dug into his denim-covered flesh.

Even when we were desperate for each other, he was always loving and gentle with me.

"I think Daddy needs to teach my boy a lesson."

"Le-lesson?"

His rough hand wrapped around the front of my throat and forced my head to rest heavier on his shoulder. The other hand grabbed the crisscrossed leather straps stretched over my chest.

"You let other men see that sexy, beautiful body of yours. You know, baby boy, that's all mine." I hissed at the slight squeeze of his hand around my throat. "You're gonna take your ass to the couch and bend over the back of it. I'm gonna spank that fat ass until it's red and hot. Then you're gonna suck Daddy's cock to show me how sorry you are."

The feral quality of his voice had my cock thickening in the minuscule scrap of fabric. I opened my mouth to tell him I'd worn my coat all night but rolled my lips between my teeth. A needy, slutty whimper sounded in my throat as he pushed me away. It wasn't hard enough to knock me off balance physically, but mentally and emotionally, I struggled at the sudden loss of his warmth and strength.

I shot him a glance as he adjusted his hard dick and raised my gaze to his.

"That's all yours, baby boy, but first you need to learn you're all mine."

It was a miracle how I made it into the living room on trembling thighs and knees. He'd spanked my ass before. During sex, playfully as I passed him somewhere in the house, but a small sliver of fear and anticipation stole my breath and sanity. As I reached the couch, I bent at the waist, popped my ass out so it was perfectly on display for my Daddy.

Every movement he made was calculated, meant to increase the tension which had turned palatable. In that moment, he was a dominant predator stalking his prey, and I locked my knees so they wouldn't collapse as he forced me to wait. He disappeared as he stepped behind me, then denim met my ass cheeks bared by my thong.

I whimpered as strong fingers knotted in my loose curls

and jerked my head back. His bigger body blanketed mine. His hot breath was teasing the whorl of my ear.

"Do you know how sexy this soft body and curves are to Daddy?" He rolled his hips, and I sunk my teeth into my bottom lip.

"Yes, Daddy." I slammed my eyes closed as he slipped his left hand between our bodies.

He tucked his fingers under the strip of fabric and gently tugged, teasing my aching, empty hole. Then his knuckles were an agonizing brush over the wrinkled skin.

"So, needy, love, tell me who this body belongs to? Who owns every whimper? Every release?"

"You do, Daddy, only you." I was surprised the words stayed strong and didn't break. "No," I yelled as his presence and touch disappeared. As I tried to straighten, he spread his hand between my shoulder blades and held me in place.

"Tell me you deserve your correction?"

"I do. I was bad."

"And why were you bad?"

Before I could answer, the sound of his palm meeting my right ass cheek stole my words with surprise, and the second one had pain and pleasure skittering along my skin. My nipples pulled achingly tight.

"I believe I asked you a question."

"I showed other people Daddy's body."

"That's right." His gravelly voice turned deeper, and I held tight to the cushions on the couch as I prepared.

The spanking intensified, heat and pain infused my bottom as he seemed to focus on the same spots repeatedly until I fought to get away. It was futile as he held me in place with the back of the couch cutting into my belly. I always wondered what it would feel like to be loved and used, to truly belong to someone, and Grey showed me how beautiful it was to be his man, boy, and slut.

He made everything okay. It made all the pieces fit

perfectly together without molding me to fit him. Because at the end of the day, every part of me notched into alignment with him.

I cried out as he reached between my spread thighs to stroke my hard, leaking dick. I humped his hand only to whine as he stopped. He rubbed his calloused hand over my spanked bottom; pain and ecstasy bloomed, and I rolled my hips into his touch.

"I think my boy liked his punishment too much."

"It was terrible, Daddy, don't do it a—" My bratty answer sharply cut off as he issued another series of smacks. This time there was no teasing or mercy. This was punishment, and I lived for it because even as he corrected me, his love and care were clear.

I collapsed as the strikes ceased, and he once again draped his body over mine. His hairy chest tickling my sweaty back, and he tenderly kissed my cheek. My mouth dropped open as his hand was back between us; his thumb massaged my hole as he rutted against me.

His free hand cupped my chin and turned my head until his lips captured mine in a kiss that was all need and no finesse. His ragged breaths through his nose blew across my cheek.

"Do you even understand how proud I am to be yours, Sugar? To know that everyone who sees me knows that my man is everything to me?"

Emotion choked me, and I couldn't answer but nodded my head. Because I knew—it was in every action, every kiss, no matter where we were or the way he held my hand or pulled me closer as we walked down the street. It was Grey and Shug, a cohesive unit without ridicule or judgment. We just were.

"I don't think you truly know, but I'm going to spend the rest of my life making sure you understand. So beautiful." He brushed his mouth to the corner of mine. "So brilliant."

Another kiss. "So sexy." His teeth nipped at my bottom lip. "So mine."

His lips caught the tear that slipped from the side of my eye and hushed me, whispered words of praise as his arm slipped around me. Cuddled me to his chest as I hiccupped sobs and let the tears fall. I'd spent years waiting and looking, at times molding myself into what society would deem acceptable, and all it had taken was a move to a small Montana town and saying hi to the stoic hardware store owner.

I didn't know how long we remained there, but I felt him straighten with me still pressed to his chest. I squeaked as he swept me into his arms and kissed me properly. His lips, tongue, and teeth teased me until I was panting, my arousal that had fled during my emotional meltdown returned.

"Let me get you upstairs, and I'll give you a nice hot bath, then we'll cuddle."

"What about the blowjob?"

"We have plenty of time for that. Holding you is much more important right now."

I knew there was a stupid grin on my face as he took my hand and led me up to his bedroom. I could regret a lot of things in life, but unknowingly waiting for Grey wasn't one of them. If we lasted another year or a lifetime, I'd cherish every second of my time.

17

GREY

"ARE YOU BEING SEXUALLY AND SPIRITUALLY FULFILLED?"

I choked on the forkful of food I'd just swallowed as Star asked. Tears filled my eyes as my boy patted my back and offered me my water. I tried to wordlessly assure him I was fine, but I was probably in the process of dying. I should've known better after two days spent with Shug's mother and her husbands.

"Mom, he's meeting all my needs, now, stop trying to kill my man."

"But, Sugar, this is important for you. There are people who find intimacy and/or sex doesn't empower them. But in your case, I know that you need a physical and emotional connection with someone. This isn't a minor issue."

"And as I said, he's meeting all my physical, emotional, and mental needs. Don't scare him off. I'd like to keep him."

I cleared my throat and took hold of his hand. I brought it to my mouth and brushed my lips across his knuckles.

"Fine, fine, I should've known you'd hook up with a *normie* and ruin all my fun."

I hid my snort as she rolled her eyes and went back to eating dinner. We'd done a vegan meal mixed with a traditional one. The previous night I'd watched my boy prep for his parents' meal, and I hadn't recognized anything he'd worked with, especially the powder he mixed in that he assured me was a meat substitute. He'd told me it wasn't awful, but I refused to try it. My adventurous nature didn't extend to the weird lump of gluten.

Thankfully the conversation went to safer topics, the community garden, mutual friends, and working to open a new shelter for homeless people to have a place to transition as they found new jobs and homes. I listened intently as Shug's input was requested, and they planned to have video calls to discuss the process. They amazed me, and I realized how much of the bond between mother and son had formed the man I'd fallen in love with. I hadn't told him, but my natural cautiousness told me he wasn't ready to hear it, or maybe I wasn't ready for his reaction to my confession.

Star's partners kicked us out of the kitchen to clean up since we'd cooked. I excused myself to deal with my horses and get them settled for the night. I was just putting down fresh hay when I sensed I wasn't alone. I turned my head to find Star watching me.

"Your quiet is making me nervous."

She chuckled and smiled. "You know I heard about you for five years. I almost believed you were a hallucination because no one could be that perfect in my son's eyes."

"He talked about me?"

"Oh yeah. I tried to convince him to make his feelings known to you a long time ago, but he went on all these dates, one after another, every one was an utter failure, and I knew in some way my son was comparing your energy to theirs."

"You're very big on energy."

"It's not in a religious way. Spiritually we all put off this aura. People would call it gut instinct, like when you meet someone, and there's the sense of fear or foreboding. Then there's people who just infuse you with a sense of safety. That's what you gave my son. As you can probably figure out, I raised my son in an untraditional way. He took a lot of bullying for that, he tried to conform, but in the end, he was miserable."

I set the pitchfork aside and watched as her eyes turned glassy with tears. I wasn't comfortable with giving her a hug or to reassure her that she'd done something right. That her son had turned out to be an amazing person.

"Sugar isn't someone who can be molded into what society deems appropriate. It's in his sexuality. His gender presentation. I didn't raise him in a home where clothes, chores, or expectations were gendered. I surrounded him with people with the same belief structure. When he mentioned the day he met you, he was in such awe that even in this small town...a man who looked like you would treat him with respect. I think you made him feel like he'd made the right decision to move here."

"He's perfect, Star. It took me a while to get myself to see what was between us. I didn't actively ignore it but did so anyway. I never saw him as this thing to consider *other*. My parents didn't raise me that way. And it's a lot more progressive here than you'd think. I respected his openness and his pride in who he was. Also, he was an exceptionally beautiful person."

"I think I liked you the minute he mentioned how you reacted to him. Whether his crush developed into anything, I was happy he had a friend in you. You don't know how hard it was for me not to do a happy dance when you answered that video call. Also, I'm not gonna lie and say the view wasn't really nice."

My cheeks heated at her waggling brows, and then her gentle laughter rang inside the barn.

"Thanks, but I only care if he enjoys the view."

"Oh, let me put your mind at ease, he's always loved it, but that isn't why I came out here. Sugar tried to talk me out of it, but it's a mother's...a parent's prerogative to ask the intentions of their children's partner or partners. You love my son. I already figured that out from simply watching your interactions. You put him first. You made his plate, poured his drink, opened his door...went above and beyond what most people would do with someone they're dating."

"I haven't told him. I don't want to say the words until the moment I tell him. We're still new as a couple, but not as friends. We've shared meals and conversations. He even hid in corners with me when I was forced to go to parties or bars. He accepted what I thought was boring and predictable. I'm not the best with words, so for me physically showing him...taking care of him is the way I communicate how I feel."

"We all have our love languages. You don't have to apologize for that. And I think you're both compatible in that way. I just wanted you to know I approve, and you make Sugar so happy. Thank you for that. I'll let you get your chores done and go put my child out of his misery. He didn't want me to come out here."

"Please, don't torture him. But, Star, thanks, I promise I'll make him happy."

"I know you will. Peace and love might be my core philosophy, but that doesn't mean I haven't made some *friends* in the past who can take care of problems."

I chuckled and shook my head as she winked at me and left me alone to finish what I needed so I could get back to my boy. Maybe a part of me was relieved she'd searched me out. Because Brenda's parents had known me forever, it was the expectation we'd marry and be a couple, have a family. Travel that traditional path that society tells you that you should want.

Winning over a parent, especially one like Star and the closeness she had with Sugar, that made it so much more profound, in the sense, I was not who she probably assumed her son would want to be with. In hers and his world, I was the *other*. That piece that never quite fit. I believed that's why he'd drawn me so much. I'd felt like the outcast even in a town and world that accepted me as a constant.

I always wanted to be Sugar's constant.

I WAS MENTALLY EXHAUSTED, BUT I HAD TO ADMIT I LIKED Star and her partners, Harry and Floyd. They doted on their wife, and Shug admitted his mother seemed a lot happier and content since she'd been with the two men. It was a true triad; the two men had been lovers when they met Star. I didn't understand it because I couldn't imagine sharing my boy with anyone. I'd even tried to picture the option because it was something he'd grown up with, but it was an impossibility.

They were happy and consenting adults, so I wouldn't judge. I watched from the entryway to the kitchen as Shug said bye to his mom and stepfathers. They'd leave the next morning to return home. His nervousness had grown over the weeks until Thanksgiving. I knew he was scared his gregarious family would scare me away. He'd learn nothing would make me say it was too much being with him.

I'd hung out with his stepfathers; they'd helped me with chores or shared tea as Star and Shug spent time together alone to catch up. Star had started giving me hugs and cheek kisses—an affection that was so easy and natural for her. I'd slowly started to realize I was going to belong to a family again.

Family was a concept I'd lost since my dad's death. I had my friends and the people in town, but it wasn't a true family —at least I didn't feel that way about them. We were a unit. A community. Yet not a family, and I wanted Shug to be that for me in whatever way. Children wasn't something I thought about as a tangible. Maybe one day we'd discuss adoption, but at that moment, I loved that he was my sole focus. I needed that for at least a while. I'd been alone so long that it was a habit I needed to break, almost like that first drink I refused all those years ago.

The door closed, and I watched him spin to lean back against it. He laid his head back on the surface, and I smiled.

"Exhausted, baby boy?" I pushed away from the frame and started to approach him. He lifted his head, and I took in the happiness of his smile as he saw me stood in front of him.

"So exhausted. Living here and not being physically present with her, I forget how much energy it requires."

"Does that mean you're not running off home any time soon?"

"You know I don't want to go anywhere, Daddy. I'm quite happy with my life, friends or lovers. I wouldn't be able to leave."

I braced myself against the door, my hands spread out on the surface above his shoulders. I lowered until I could slant my mouth across his. He instantly curled his hands in the sides of my shirt. As we kissed, he pushed up on his toes and deepened the kiss. A growl rumbled in my chest.

"Ready for bed?"

"Beyond ready, I didn't get my morning cuddles. I'm sorry about that."

"It's okay. I could've done without waking up with your mother staring at me from the other side of the bed."

He giggled, and all I could remember was the thankfulness I'd dressed in pajama bottoms.

"I'm sorry. You had to put up with a lot by agreeing to host my family for dinner."

I held onto his hands as I backed up to the stairs, led him to the bedroom to get him undressed and changed for bed. When he was with me, he knew his every need or want was mine to give him. I bathed or dressed, prepared him dinner, and sometimes fed him because I loved the blush he got when he realized how much of my attention was only for him.

"I don't see it as putting up with anything. Your family is

important, and if I want to see where this goes, we need to at least know I can co-exist with yours."

"Doesn't mean I didn't feel badly about her *letting* herself in."

"You could've mentioned her burglar skills."

"Shady pasts come after you start liking her more." I stripped him of his tunic he wore over a pair of black leggings.

I slowly exposed his beautiful body. His suppleness, lightly tanned skin and smooth body was the sexiest thing I'd ever seen in my life. Physically I couldn't complain about an inch of his form. Yet it wasn't about how much the physical presence of him excited me. No, it was the confidence in which he carried everything the world would consider a flaw. Silvery stretch marks on his stomach and hips, and more scattered here and there. I'd kissed and licked every one of his beautiful imperfections. The roundness of his chest and belly, his body was built to cushion my larger, harder one.

"Let's go to bed so I can hold you. I haven't kissed you like I've wanted to all day. I crave it so much."

He turned away from me to turn down the bed. Presented with his lush ass, I groaned as I removed my own clothes. By the time I slipped into bed, he was already cuddled under the covers, his head on my pillow. We wouldn't sleep any time soon, but he understood that holding him brought each of us peace. And we'd never deny the other that comfort.

18

GREY

SHUG GIGGLED AS I GRABBED HIS HAND AND TUGGED HIM behind the counter, into the backroom where we could have privacy. I wanted a real kiss, not the ones I kept g-rated in public. The longer we were together, the higher my sex drive became, and it seemed my body was trying to make up for years of abstinence, or more than likely, I just couldn't get enough of my boy.

"Grey, we can't—"

I shut him up by coming up behind him, and pressed my body close to his and roughly shoved his skirt up and his thick striped tights down to expose the tanned, dimpled curves of his ass. The door was open, the closed sign was turned, but the front door was still unlocked. Anyone could come in, but I couldn't control my need for the man I'd come to love. He was mine. He made sure I knew he was mine, and I showed him I belonged to him as well.

He turned his head; his rounded cheeks reddened, and his plump lips parted. I pushed my hands under his shirt to play with his nipples as I kissed him, rutted against his ass. He sucked at my tongue. Every day that passed where our relationship grew, the more I craved him. Going a day without possessing or being able to touch him was unbearable for me.

"Fuck, baby boy, I've been hard since you came by for your morning kiss." My hands shook as I unbuckled my belt, popped the button loose, and unzipped my jeans. "Arms above your head, boy, don't make me bind them." I pushed my pants and briefs down. He whimpered as my cock notched between his ass cheeks.

His submission to my order made me growl as I nipped at his ear and found the small bottle of lube.

"Daddy, please." I slicked my cock and then added more lube to my fingers as I prepped him quickly, had him quickly riding two of my thick fingers as I spread the lube around the inside of his contracting hole. It didn't matter how many times I loved on him in my bed or his. I'd never had this feral compulsion with anyone but him. He was made for me in every way.

Fucking him was like coming home. Normally, I teased and seduced until he was mindless with need for me, but times like this, I was too far gone to love on him. I wiped my hand, wrapped my fingers around the base, and lined up.

"You ready for me? Tell Daddy what belongs to me."

"I do, Daddy. Only yours."

"Assume the position," I ordered, and he shifted backward to present me with his exposed ass. We'd both gotten tested a month after we started dating. I couldn't stand a barrier between us. I looked down to see his waxed hole slightly swollen from me stretching him. When I placed the head of my cock and pushed, he jerked and I smacked his hip to warn him to be still. "You get Daddy's dick when I say you do. Do you understand me, boy?"

"S-sorry." His voice trembled and then he softly moaned as his body opened to accept my thickness. I shallowly fucked him, giving him inch by inch. Never my entire cock. I lifted my gaze to his face, and his cheek was pressed to the wall while tears slipped from the corner of his eye.

"Pull those sexy cheeks apart for me."

He reached back and grabbed them, parted them, and I groaned as I watched his long dark purple nails sink into his skin.

"You were made to be my slutty, little boy, weren't you?" I asked but didn't give him time to respond as I finally thrust until my pelvis met his ass, setting off the jiggle of his flesh. There was something about the softness, the movement of his curves as I fucked him that dangerously pushed me to the edge of my control. "Don't make a sound...you don't want us to get caught. Your sounds and the way you look on Daddy's cock is only for me."

I curved my hands over his shoulders as his hole strangled my dick, braced him as my hips pulled back and then I used his slick hole. The sounds of his well-lubed hole taking my cock, the jangle of my buckle, and his muffled little grunts. My muscles strained as I used him because he was mine. No one else would ever be able to love on him — call him theirs.

"Daddy's perfect boy." I hissed through my teeth as his ass clamped down and I forced my way in and out of the sudden vice as I angled for that spot again. I knew just where and how he liked me to pound his hard little gland. I leaned over him, my lips to his ear. "Mine. I waited so long for you."

The bell went off out front. "Fuck, jack that pretty cock, I'm not stopping until you come on my cock. Give your Daddy what he needs." I straightened a bit. "Be right with you," I called out and was thankful my voice sounded almost normal and lowered my mouth back to his ear as he shook and bit back whimpers as he did what his Daddy asked.

"Fuck, boy, work for your reward. Daddy's come in that tight—" I wrapped my arm around him, my forearm and hand sinking into the softness of his belly as his body bowed and he came hard. I thrust so hard he had to brace one hand on the wall as I pounded him until I sealed my hips to his ass and gave him everything I had. I straightened and slipped free, my seed leaking out as I rubbed his poor, abused hole. "Stay back here until my customer is gone." I pulled him up and turned him to drop my mouth to his. "You made Daddy so proud, baby boy."

"Thank you, Daddy."

It took every ounce of self-control I possessed to head to the bathroom and wash lube and come from my cock and balls. I made sure I was presentable and closed the door so he could move around freely as he worked on washing up and fixing his clothes.

"Mr. Carson, how are you today?" The little elderly man smiled as he moved around with the help of his cane.

"Good, good, the missus wants to paint the bedroom again."

"Your son going to take care of it for you? I could—"

"No, no, he's going to do it. You're always so quick to volunteer. You have to focus on keeping that young man of yours happy."

"It's all I focus on, Mr. Carson."

"Not all of us get lucky enough to find a good person."

I smiled. "No, we don't. Did your wife have a color picked out?" As I asked, he handed over the color chip and told me how many gallons he needed. "You need it today or want to pick it up later?"

"My son will be by Friday to pick it up after he gets off work, that okay?"

"Perfect, I'll just do an order for you." I went through the motions of filling out the invoice, he gave me his card, and I ran it. Before long, he was on his way with a receipt, and I placed my copy in the holder to mix Friday. I made my way into the backroom to find Shug seated on my desk, looking gorgeous and well-loved. Crossing the room, I slipped between his thighs and lowered my mouth to his. He hugged my waist as I brushed my lips to his.

"Do you know how much I love you?"

He jerked back and stared up at me with wide eyes. "What?"

"Is it such a shock? I haven't shown you you're mine?"

"You really love me?" His voice broke over the question.

"I do, maybe I should've done the whole dinner and flowers, kissed you at the door and told you, but I wasn't lying when I said I'd waited so long for you. My person may not have come in the package I expected. At my age, I'd given up on finding anyone. To think you walked into my store five years ago, on those sexy heels and with a flirty smile, maybe I sensed it back then." I lifted my hands to cup his stubble-covered jaw and stroked my thumbs over his lips. "There was always something about you I couldn't quite deny, the way I craved your company during our lunches and the time we spent together alone in a corner. The night of your birthday, watching another man touch you, I didn't understand the protectiveness or possessiveness. I'd never felt that for anyone, man or woman."

"I love you, too. I fell so hard, and I denied it because I knew I couldn't have a man like you. What happens now?"

"We've only been seeing each other a short time, but one day if you don't get sick of me, I want you to move all your chaos in with me. Mix your life with mine. Make my home yours. Would you like that?"

"I really would."

"Your lunch break is almost up; I'm going to order you lunch to be delivered to the shop. Spend the night with me." I nipped at his lower lip. "Hate sleeping without you, baby boy."

"Want me to meet you at home?"

"No, I'll pick you up, we're supposed to get snow tonight, and I don't want you driving in it."

"Okay." He agreed so easily.

"No argument?"

"Why would I argue with you wanting me safe? Daddy, I

love you taking care of me. The way you're a gentleman because it's natural for you. The lunchtime quickie was a surprise."

I loved his little smirk and the way he leaned into me. "You just make me lose control, and I'm not used to that. I couldn't imagine not being your man and Daddy."

He whined. "I have to get back to work. There're a few samples coming this afternoon. New garter belts and stockings. They're in my size."

"I think you need to bring them tonight." He giggled as I dropped another kiss to his lips and reluctantly let him go. I gave him a quick hug and then closed my eyes to listen to the tap of his heels on the floor. His *I love you* still played in my head.

There were a few questions I'd held off on asking. I wanted to know what he thought about marriage and kids. The one time we'd discussed kids, he hadn't seemed as if he wanted any, and that was fine. It wasn't something I'd even thought about when I was married. The marriage part, I wanted that with him one day. Everyone in town knew he was mine, and there hadn't even been shock when we'd gone public on our first date. All we heard was it was about time.

When he was ready, I wanted my ring on his finger, his touches around my home, and I knew we'd have all of that. He was everything I wanted and some things I hadn't even anticipated, and I'd make sure he never doubted my love for him.

19

SHUG

HE LOVED ME. EVEN A FEW WEEKS LATER, THE WORDS echoing in my head still shocked me. I'd never doubted he cared for me. He showed me in everything he did, but love? That old, bullied teenager in me or the adult who just couldn't keep a boyfriend urged me to be careful. I didn't want to be cautious.

Being with Grey was everything and more than I'd ever imagined it would be. I stared across the small table at Mean Bean Coffee and Café at Carlos as we hung out for lunch. Drew had an issue, and Grey had taken off to help him.

"So, it seems you're alive."

"Don't be an asshole. You knew I was alive." I sipped at my coffee and tried not to smile at the perturbed expression on my friend's face.

Before Grey, we'd had coffee a few times a week, and I always showed up to Shane's for drinks. I didn't even have an issue that things had changed. Grey never stopped me from going out because he wouldn't like sitting at a bar while everyone drank, and he'd have to act as designated driver. Not that he'd complain, it was a tradition leftover from his dad, and he wanted to carry it on.

No, my man just didn't want me to be uncomfortable and to just let go for a night, and then I'd call him to come pick me up. I'd walk out into the night to find him leaned back against his truck, a smile for me as he opened the passenger door. No, the routine didn't bore me as I knew he worried.

"How's reality living up to fantasy? You waited a long time for our clueless Grey to notice."

"I don't know. I mean, reality is better, but that small cynic that lives in the back of my brain waited for him to figure out what being with me would mean."

"You're a moron." He laughed as he relaxed back in his chair and crossed his legs.

"Hey, that's not nice."

"You are. Grey has lived in this town for forty years except for his foray into the world of big city college life. It wasn't lost on us that he changed a bit after you moved here. He smiled more. Willingly spent time with you. For fuck's sake, he talked to you. Conversations with him were only slightly better than grunts and head shakes or nods."

"I can't imagine him that way. He's so sweet and open, affectionate. The man I see isn't the one described to me."

That was true for the most part. From the second I'd met Grey, he was friendly. Yes, I noticed he was a bit quiet, but some people were just naturally reserved. It had been in the way he was always buttoned up. He'd always made me feel at home. I couldn't reconcile the stories I heard with the man I knew.

"Believe it, honey. Brenda did him wrong in so many ways. His cluelessness wasn't something new. She ran around on him hard, a lot more than the one she ran off with."

I didn't tell him that I didn't think Grey was as clueless about his cheating wife as everyone assumed. "How could anyone cheat on him?" I'd been cheated on a few times, even with an understanding that open or Poly relationships didn't bother me. That was back before I realized I wasn't a sharer like my mother. I knew the pain infidelity caused when a simple conversation could lessen the hurt.

"It was easy. Brenda went off to college. Lived a life far removed from what was in Jenkins. She did what she wanted, but since she wasn't willing to work to stay in the city...she came home. Married Grey because, like in most small towns, the quarterback marries the head cheerleader, and they live happily ever after."

"Are there any pictures of Grey in a football uniform?"

"You've got it so bad. You're thinking about quarterback and cheer squad captain roleplay, aren't you?"

"I wasn't." I giggled as he groaned and threw his head back.

He lifted his head to look at me. "You know I'm happy for you, right?"

"Yeah, you and everyone have been the best about not outing me and my secret crush. I was worried about scaring him away."

"I know you did, honey, but why do you think we made sure Drew would bring him to Shane's or parties at the Orchard or even the cookouts and stuff? We were playing matchmaker. The first time you two disappeared to the side to huddle and talk, the betting pools started."

"That wasn't uncomfortable at all during our first date."

He let out a loud bark of laughter and everyone turned to look, and I rolled my eyes as he held his stomach. I hope he pissed himself. Were the bets still going? Jenny had said marriage or moving in was next on the sheet. As much as I loved and adored Grey, I didn't know about the marriage thing. Not that I'd say no if he asked, but I'd heard the stories of his parents and grandparents, how did a couple live up to what amounted to fairy tales. Also, before I'd moved to Jenkins, monogamy wasn't practiced by my family and friend groups.

Grey had committed to his vows so fully that he'd remained

in a loveless union, and I never wanted to put my man through that. Dammit, I had to get over that. He loved me. I believed it. Yet, I wanted to be positive I could make him happy for the long term prior to sealing our commitment in that way.

"Shug, Shug, Shug, have you not figured out it yet? This town is small. All we have is gossip and drama, and you and Grey have given this town a wealth of gossip in the last five years."

"Did people have an issue with me when I moved here?"

He shook his head. "No, when I met Simon when he was on business in L.A. Oh my god, when I learned he lived in Montana, I thought he was a complete closet case. I thought one night was all we'd have. He asked me for my number." He placed his forearms on the table and leaned forward. "I gave it to him but never once thought I'd hear from him again. He called me from the airport...when he landed, when he got home, and texts and calls daily after that. To me, it wasn't anything serious. We'd flirt or have some phone sex. I freaked out the first time he asked me to come visit him."

"But you came."

"I did, but he had to beg me for six months before I agreed."

"How long before you moved here?"

He grinned and shook his head. "I never left."

"Never?"

"Well, I had to pack up my apartment. The first night I was here after he picked me up at the airport, we went to The Orchard for dinner. He kissed me at the table like it was normal. We went to Shane's the next night. He introduced me to everyone as his boyfriend, and no one even flinched."

"I think that's one of the things I noticed. That first week I was freaking out that I'd made the fuck-up of the century. The first day I had to venture out, I dressed as I normally would. I had a now or never attitude about it."

"And the first place you go is the hardware store."

"I needed paint." I really hadn't needed paint that badly, but it was mid-morning, and it was the place that looked the least busy.

"Uh-huh. Is that the story you're sticking with?"

"It wasn't busy in there, less people to stare at me, but when I saw the sexy man behind the counter, I wasn't complaining."

He opened his mouth to give me shit—I knew that was his intention—but his phone beeped. He dug into the inside pocket of his coat and pulled it out. The smile on his face told me it was his husband. Si and he were the first couple I'd started hanging out with after I moved to town. Carlos had stopped into my shop to introduce himself and told me about Shane's and caught me up on gossip and the places to be in Jenkins.

"You have to go?"

"Yes, we're going away to a bed and breakfast for an overnight to have some alone time. Don't be a damn stranger, just because you got a man now, remember you still have friends."

"I will, I promise. Sorry."

"Don't be sorry. We all have the honeymoon phase. You need to work a bit to get Grey out of his comfort zone. He's locked himself up far too long."

"I'll work on it, I promise."

I stood, we kissed each other's cheeks, and I sat back down to finish my coffee. Grey's last text said he wouldn't be home until dinner time. Drew's landlord did the bare minimum in maintenance. He'd told me to head to his place and he'd make dinner, but I wanted to get there first.

Grey took care of everyone else, and I wanted the opportunity to spoil him a bit. I'd start with dinner and maybe a massage since he worked so hard that day. As much as I knew he didn't require or expect to be made a priority, in no way would I spend our relationship letting him go above and beyond our entire time together.

I'd make sure my man—my Daddy—knew how much he meant to me. He deserved all the good things I could give him. Especially when he always put himself last.

20

GREY

ALL DAY I'D SLOWLY WORKED THROUGH DREW'S GREY-TO-do list, and that's why I was sprawled on his kitchen floor with my head stuck under the sink replacing the garbage disposal. I'd told my best friend to find a house since he'd pay for maintenance anyway.

"What's left on this damn list?" I asked as I tightened the couplings and grimaced as I tried to contort my broad shoulders in the cramped space. I was giving my boy a spanking on principle alone; he'd urged me to come help Drew.

As thoughts of Shug filled my head, I wondered what he was doing. If he was still with Carlos or at my house where he belonged, waiting for me to come home?

"I think that's everything except for the tile in the bathroom. You're supposed to check to see if it's water damage or if the broken ones can just be replaced. I think you can leave Shug's poor ass alone for a few hours."

I growled under the sink. "Get my boy's ass out of your head."

"Possessive? When did my stoic best friend become all Alpha male?"

The corner of my mouth pulled into a smirk. I enjoyed the

newness of being me. No one other than Shug knew the intent I'd protected myself with the reserved attitude. Or how I ignored my dominant sexual needs.

"If you even pop a hard-on right now, I'm kicking you out."

"Give me a few minutes of thinking of my boy, and I'll get out of your way."

"You're a disgusting man, Grey Callaghan."

I chuckled loudly and finished up under the sink and slid out. I tightened my abdomen and sat up to find Drew glaring at me. My drama queen of a friend never changed. I didn't want him to. Through my college meltdown, fucked-up marriage, and the aftermath, he'd always stood beside me.

"Shug has corrupted you."

"If you ask him, he'd probably give you the opposite answer."

He frantically waved his hands. "No, no, we made a promise a long time ago, we'd never discuss sex or conquests, or what-the-fuck-ever."

"When did you turn into a prude?"

"When the hell did you turn into a freak? And don't think I haven't noticed our beautiful Shug using Daddy to address you."

"You should hear him scream it."

I got to my feet and straightened as he covered his ears and yelled. Pushing his buttons became easier every year. I think my best friend's maturity levels were progressing in reverse. I circled his wrists and pulled his arms down. I released him and went about cleaning up my tools.

"You need to relax." My voice clearly showed my amusement, and I didn't bother to restrain it. I'd always assumed I was, if not happy, I was at least content with my life. Yet, I'd spent over fifteen years lying to myself. A few years after reciting my vows, I'd believed it was forever, but it wasn't. With Shug, regret wouldn't play a role in my feelings for him.

When I looked back to analyze how it had all imploded, I

realized I'd let it happen. I didn't fight for my marriage or all the dreams I had for my life. As with all the years and milestones, I'd acquiesced with an ease that shamed me. In all honesty, I hadn't believed my ex-wife was worth fighting for. There wasn't a sliver of our relationship we could've salvaged.

"Grey?"

"Yeah?" I asked absentmindedly.

"You're happy, right?"

"Extremely."

"Are you sure?"

"What the hell is that supposed to mean?" I turned to glare at him.

"It's not an insult. There's always something I've known about you. You're adaptable to a point. When Brenda cheated on you, you didn't seem affected in any way. When the divorce became final, you went to work the next day like it was any other. You were your normal, polite, and reserved self. Would it be the same if that was Shug?"

I knew the answer, and it was easy. "It would destroy me."

"Why is that?" he asked, as he moved to the opposite side of the island and bent over to rest on his forearms.

"Brenda and I dated for three years. She was my first. Maybe I was hers, who knows. We went through the motions of small-town romance. We were a habit...a routine. Then college came around, and instead of screwing with the status quo, we decided we'd go our separate ways, and when college was over, we'd discuss getting married. I think if we'd actually been in love, teenagers or not, we'd have fought for and adapted to the long-distance thing."

"Then why didn't you just leave it at that, then?"

"Because we were twenty-two years old, and Brenda's parents were old-fashioned. They had expectations. They assumed their precious daughter was studying and saving herself to come home and get married. My dad wasn't clueless. Dad sat me down the first summer I was home to talk to me.

I'd lost weight, and he could tell it wasn't just about adjusting to college life. Dad would've told me not to marry her. That my happiness was more important, but the stories I heard about my grandparents, what I remembered and was told about my parent's romance, it was always solid even when they fought. I was successful in everything I ever did except that one area."

"Did you think something was wrong with you?"

"Maybe. I always asked myself what did I do wrong? Did I not give her something she needed? What about me disgusted her so much she couldn't bear my touch and went elsewhere? But you know, she cheated on me for years. I just had to learn to not view it as something I did wrong or she did wrong. We caved to expectations. We were both at fault and innocent at the same time. I can believe we would've remained friends if we were honest with each other."

I'd spent so much time questioning myself. Going over the what-ifs and dissecting all my decisions and actions. If we'd moved away like she wanted, would we have had that perfect suburban life; the white picket fence and the kids? I wasn't going to torture myself any longer. It worked out the way it did, and in the end, I got Shug, and he was my gift.

"You got something on your mind, Drew?"

"Not really. I just wondered why it was so easy for you. One day you're this confirmed heterosexual bachelor, and suddenly, you're a proud bisexual man with an adorable boyfriend. To everyone else, I'm this slightly flighty man, moving from one person to the next, always searching, but I question everything. Personality-wise, that should've been you."

I studied the hint of sadness and loneliness on my best friend's handsome face. Maybe I wasn't the only one who excelled at masking my emotions and insecurities. I mirrored his position and looked him in the eyes.

"I questioned, but I'm this strange mix of insecure and highly self-aware. Shug always threw me for this strange, dizzying loop since the day he walked into my store. Now, don't get me wrong, I wasn't carrying some secret torch for years. No, I noticed he made me feel off. He shook me up where no one else ever could. You know how I grew up." He nodded. "Bigotry wasn't taught in my house, so I never viewed different sexualities or gender identities as this thing to cause me to view people for their otherness." I paused to try to find the right words. "Then, as time passed and he became my friend, I noticed how much I craved his company. He broke up the isolation I felt, and I started noticing I loved the way he expressed himself, his independence, and then I started noticing how beautiful he was. At its core, it wasn't easy but claiming him was."

He nodded and smiled at me.

"I'm happy for you, Grey. I'm also glad it worked out for him, too. Because not having you was killing him inside."

"Let's take a look at the tile so I can get home."

I finished up the list and made a list of what I needed to fix the broken tiles. I told him I'd be by the next weekend to repair them, picked up my toolbox, and on my way to my truck, I sent my boy a text to let him know I was on my way home.

21

SHUG

I HADN'T EVEN BOTHERED GOING TO MY HOUSE BECAUSE IT no longer felt like home. A lot of my clothes and books, personal items had made it to Grey's place. Holidays were at his place. Saturday nights, he took me out to dinner, whether that was in town or we took rides and stopped wherever. Weekends spent curled up on the couch or in bed, long talks about anything and everything. Plans for the future. I knew he still worried that what he called his boring life would send me running, but I had no intention of doing that.

We'd even discussed kids one night, but we both decided we'd wait a while to make that decision. Not that Grey wouldn't make an amazing dad, but I was unsure about how I'd do. Would I cause a repeat of the cycle of bullying on a child because he belonged to me? Would they be embarrassed one of their dads would show up in heels, skirts, or just make-up? I made choices in my life, and I didn't want someone to suffer for them. Especially when I only did them to make me happy.

He'd tried to put my fears to rest and told me whatever decision I made was fine with him. I'd searched for disappointment. Yet all I'd seen was honesty. He'd be happy with or without us raising children together. I just needed to be ready, and whenever that happened, all I had to do was tell him.

As soon as I walked inside, not a lot of lights were on inside, which was odd. Daddy would've been home nearly an hour already. I hung the strap of my bag on the coat rack and removed my jacket to join it. My heels clicked on the hardwood floors as I searched for him.

The living room lamp was on low. "Grey, are you home?" He had to be around somewhere since his truck was there. Maybe he was still out with the horses. He didn't answer, so I headed for the kitchen to finish whatever dinner he'd started. Valentine's day was coming up soon, and like most gift-giving holidays, my online store turned busy.

We'd missed out on nights together. He tried to soothe my guilt over feeling as if I was ignoring him when he did so much to spend time with me. If I needed to deal with shipping orders, he'd arrive with takeout from my favorite places and share a meal. Every night he'd call me to tell me goodnight. I froze in the entryway into the kitchen. Grey stood there in a pair of worn jeans and a dress shirt, the sleeves rolled up and the top two buttons undone. At work, he was still completely buttoned-up and stoic, but for me, he let down his guard. He also knew I had a weakness for that little triangle of hairy skin exposed by his unbuttoned shirt. After months together, I knew every inch of his body. I'd kissed every scar and mole, the small birthmark he had on his left shoulder blade.

The table beside him was set, and candles were lit.

He grinned at me. "Hi, baby boy." He motioned me forward, and I didn't hesitate to walk into his arms.

"What are you up to, Daddy?" Like always, I melted into him, inhaling the scent of his subtle cologne. I sighed as he hugged me closer, and every bit of stress eased away.

"You've been working so hard I thought you needed a night of being pampered. I made you dinner. I'll fill the tub to let you relax. A massage if you've been a really good boy."

I eased away and tried to straighten my glasses, and he instantly fixed them for me. Long days killed my eyes, so I wore them more when I was busy and all the time at home.

"I made lasagna and conned Tony out of his tiramisu recipe."

"Aw, Tony guards that recipe with his life and threats of being haunted by his grandmother."

"It took some convincing. But before we eat, there's something I want to talk to you about."

A talk with anyone else would've sent me into a panic, but this was Grey, my Daddy, and he'd never do anything to hurt me or make a meal to lessen the emotional blow.

"Okay, are you okay?"

"I will be. We've been dating for months now. And we exchanged the I love yous, and I met the parents."

"My mother loves you. She'd add you to the triad, but she'd have to fight me."

His rich, husky laughter made heat infuse my chest. He struggled to relax the image he had for the outside world. Not to say he didn't let everyone know how much joy I brought him, but he still was that stoic and reserved gentleman, but he was different with me.

"You wouldn't have to fight too hard. I love you too much to think anyone would be better than you. What this is about is I want you to move in. Completely. Not just your toiletries in my bathroom and your books and e-reader on the nightstand on your side of the bed. I want you to move all that beautiful chaos into my home full-time. To always know I'll come home to you or be here when you walk through the door. I know marriage and kids aren't on your list of needs." He stopped my protests with a quick kiss. "No arguing. I was married, it didn't make me happy. Kids are an abstract concept. It's not a need for me. All I want is you.

"This place was my parents' house. They shared so much love inside these walls, and I want that with you. So, I want you to think about it. You don't have to move in tomorrow or this weekend. No, whenever you're ready, I want to move you in. Make this place bright and happy. Infuse it with everything that you are. Would you want that one day soon?"

"My house doesn't feel like home anymore. It's a great house, but it's the one I picked because I needed somewhere to live. You haven't noticed I rarely go there first?"

He looped his arms around my waist and arched my body into his. His solid strength became an addiction. His love and care were everything I'd dreamed of when I'd thought about settling down. Even if he never uttered the L-word, it existed in every action of making me dinner, rubbing my feet, or a simple cuddle. It was there in every syllable he'd spoken to me.

"No, I noticed, that's why I wanted to ask. I want this to be home. Baby boy, I want to be your home just like you're mine."

I stood there staring at him. For a man who thought he was boring—one who thought he'd always be uninteresting to someone—the man was romantic as hell. He made everything perfect for me. He wanted me to be his home, and that's all I wanted.

"Do you think you're ready for my bright colors and chaotic style to mix with yours?"

"I've been ready. I loathe our nights apart. Which I know are rare, but even one has become unbearable until I can see you in the morning. Are you going to put me out of my misery and tell me I'm not making an old fool of myself?"

"I wouldn't want anything else. You could never go too fast for me. We've been dancing around this for five years. If you'd noticed me as a potential partner the day we'd met, I would've said yes to a date. But this is how it worked out, and it's right. So yes, I'll move all my chaos in."

I squeaked as his mouth slammed down on mine and his arms tightened around my waist. He easily lifted me off my feet. My legs twined around his waist. I broke the kiss.

"Where are we going? You made me dinner."

"Dinner can wait. We'll have it in bed later."

I giggled as he made it to his bedroom and dropped me onto the mattress. He straightened to study me. It wasn't like other men had. He saw me. The person I was, and in his eyes, I was just right because I was his person. After he recognized his attraction, he hadn't hesitated or questioned. He never made me feel as if it was wrong to suddenly want me.

"I love you more than anything, Sugar."

"I love you, too, Grey. Thank you for wanting to keep me."

He leaned forward, pushing his fists into the bed, and crawled up the bed until he loomed over me. His gaze locked on mine.

"No, baby boy, thank you for wanting to keep me."

Any words were left for later. We'd confessed all that we needed to. All that was left was loving on each other and starting the beginning of the rest of our futures together. However, that worked out, we'd always be us. Two pieces that should've never fit, but in the end, we had.

EPILOGUE

GREY

His TANNED SKIN WAS DAMP WITH SWEAT, AND HIS
breathing was ragged as he writhed where he was seated on
my crossed legs with his loosely wrapped around my waist in
the middle of our bed. My cock was so hard it was almost
painful, but I ignored it because as much as I wanted to fuck
him, loving on him at that moment was more important. I laced
my fingers with his and brought his left hand up to brush my
lips over the thick, platinum band around his ring finger.

A year of marriage, and I couldn't imagine a day without
him. I played with him slowly, tracing his softness with the
rough tips of my fingers, squeezing the curve of his belly and
thigh. Groaning at the sight of my hand sinking into all that
beautifully curved flesh. Kisses had long turned his lips swollen
and red, our stubble rasping together.

He whined and pouted as I tapped the base of the plug I'd
put in after I'd fed him lunch and bathed him. I praised him.
Told him everything I loved about him. How lucky I was to
have such a sweet Daddy's boy. Sweat drenched us both, and
his hair hung wet around his flushed face.

"Baby boy, do you know how proud you make Daddy?"

"Yes, Daddy." He tipped his head back as I nudged his chin

with my nose and licked down the front of his throat, to his upper chest where I bit and sucked until his beautiful skin bore my marks. I cupped the soft curves of his chest, sucked at his puffy nipples, and tugged at the little bars.

I smirked as his cock jerked against my belly and his copious amount of pre-cum mixed in with my sweat-slicked belly hair. If he got off from the minimal friction I allowed, he knew that we'd start all over again. These moments of intimacy where neither of us strived for release were what I lived for. He'd adjusted to my compulsion to edge him until he couldn't take another second.

I loved on him for hours. Days of teasing him with touches, kisses and he knew how much the lushness of him called to me. When he displayed all that plushness for me, he knew that he was everything I'd ever wanted and dreamed of, no matter his gender. He was mine in every way.

I loved and owned him. And that went both ways. He loved me, and everything I was, belonged to him.

He was whining and shaking, begging me to take him. I eased the plug from his tight, little hole.

"Lift up, baby boy, show Daddy how much you crave me." I wrapped my hand around my cock and lined up, then he lowered to take a few inches.

He threw his head back, and the trembling of his form showed me how on edge he was. The desire to throw him to the bed and fuck him until I branded every part of him as mine was riding me hard.

"Daddy."

"That's right, take a little more. You can do it. I know it feels so good. You're so tight and hot." I pushed the words past my clenched teeth. Control was something I prided myself on, but when it came to him, I rode the razor edge. As much as I edged him, it was as intense for myself.

When his lush bottom landed on my thighs, I gripped his soft hips and started a slow, easy rhythm. Sweat stung my eyes, drops tickled down the indent of my spine. I pressed my mouth to his, our tongues teasing as I increased the pace of him riding my cock until he was babbling and begging at the top of his lungs.

"That's right, come on Daddy's cock. Work for your reward, baby boy."

I clenched my jaw as pleasure tensed every muscle in my body. I buried my face against his throat as he rode my cock, squeezing and releasing as he bounced faster and harder. I grunted as I hugged him as he rutted against my belly until the heat of his release met the sweat and pre-cum.

I rolled until his body was under mine, and I pounded him, my skin slapping against his. Lust and sex thick in our bedroom.

"Harder, Daddy, fuck, make it hurt."

And I did just as he asked. I used him until his long nails tore at my back. My skin would be bloody by the time I was done with him, but I didn't care. I'd wear my boy's marks proudly. Fire burned in my muscles and my balls ached, then drew up tight as I sealed my hips to his ass and spilled inside my husband's abused hole. I shallowly fucked him as I kissed him with words of praise mixed in as I eased him down.

He needed to be soothed after so long of being loved and teased—after hours of his mind and body had been pushed to the limits of the pleasure he could handle.

"I love you, Daddy."

"I love you, too, boy."

As his stomach protested that we hadn't eaten since lunch, he giggled, and I chuckled.

"Let me shower and feed you. You need food and something to drink."

He held on tight as I tried to withdraw, and I kissed his contented smile and finally eased from the bed to go to take a shower. I'd taken care of his sexual and emotional needs; all that was left was nurturing his body.

ROUGHLY DRYING MY HAIR, I WALKED OUT OF THE bathroom after my quick shower. I tossed the towel aside and sat down on the edge of the bed. I lowered my head until I could brush my lips to his shoulder. "That didn't take long."

"Baby, I filled the tub for you. Have a nice bath and come down, and I'll make us dinner." He lifted onto his forearms, and I brushed my lips to his as I combed my fingers through his sweaty curls. "Take as long as you want. Dinner will be ready."

"Thank you, Daddy."

"You're welcome."

Getting up from the bed, I exited my bedroom, and I jogged downstairs. When I got to the kitchen, I busted out laughing at my best friend chugging water with his face bright red. That proved how long he'd hung out in our house until I'd come downstairs. I refused to allow my boy to be quiet when I loved on him.

"Hello to you, nice of you to call."

"I didn't need to hear my best friend balls deep with another one of my friends screaming Daddy. Come on, man."

"We've been going for about two hours. There was going to be no stopping. Not even if we had an audience and maybe knock next time."

He did a slow pan in my directions. "Two hours?"

"Yeah." I shrugged and went to the fridge. I'd prefer to make my boy a full dinner, but we had plenty of leftovers for both of us to be lazy for the evening. Sundays, we had an unspoken rule that other than me taking care of chores outside, these were days to spend alone.

"Are you a fucking machine?" I snorted, and he glared at me.

"Sorry, please continue."

"And why didn't I know about this?"

"I thought our sex lives weren't up for discussion." I'd walked in on Drew one time, and after that, we'd made a decision that sex was off-limits no matter if some friends shared conquests or not. He wouldn't hear stories about my husband.

"Yeah, but, wait, what do you do for two hours?"

I rolled my eyes as I pushed him away from the fridge and opened it. "You staying for dinner?"

"You're ignoring my question. How does Shug walk?"

"You do know that intimacy and sex have nothing to do with penetration, right?"

I wasn't wasting my time explaining intimacy to a grown-ass man who had way more sexual history than I did. I found some pasta salad and a roasted chicken I could slice for sandwiches.

"Whatever. I wanted to check-in. You being all in love and abandoning me."

"I won't apologize. You know where to find me. It's been a year. You should be used to it by now."

"Where's Shug?"

"I filled the bathtub for him and told him to take a bath, relax, and dinner would be ready when he got down here."

"Can I ask you something, and you not get pissed about it?"

"When have I ever gotten pissed?"

"That is true. How did you know Shug was the one?"

"Is that what you want to know or why after being friends for more than half our lives, you weren't the one?"

He choked on a sharp laugh. "I'm an asshole but not that much of one. I just want to know why him, were there men before?"

"No, no men before. Do you know what it's like to meet someone and the minute you set eyes on them, it's like this weight disappears? Or you feel a peace so complete that the lightness of it makes you dizzy?"

Drew shook his head as he took another swallow of his water.

"It wasn't instant, yes, I felt this connection with Sugar, but it so much more profound. It was the sense of instant belonging. A possessiveness I never felt before the night of his birthday. It was that chill of fear when you told me he was sick. That he was suffering, and I wasn't there to take care of him. Slowly I realized how much I wanted to know what it was like to kiss him...not just anyone...just him. Holding him as he slept was the most right I'd ever felt. It had nothing to do with his gender. It was him being him. His pride. His humor. His uniqueness. All of him is a lure, and I won't question why I fell in love with him. I just know that I do, more than anything."

I looked up from where I'd started carving the chicken to find him studying me as if he'd never seen me before. Our time together wasn't as extensive as it had been over our friendship. I also knew he was living with his new boyfriend. Settled into life in another city. Did he see me differently and judge me on that?

"I'm happy for you, Grey. You always wanted what your parents had, and it looks like you found it."

The soft clearing of a throat drew my attention to the entryway to find Shug in his hot pink caftan and his curls damp and pushed back from his face.

"I did. My parents would've loved him."

Shug moved across the kitchen until he could wrap his arms around my waist from behind. He gave me a tight squeeze, and I knew he'd heard everything I said. No matter how many times I told him, sometimes I felt he still wondered why a man like me had chosen him. But honestly, who else in the world would I ever love more than my sweet Shug?

ACKNOWLEDGMENTS

There's several people I'd love to give a special thanks for putting up with me during the writing of this super sweet, toothache-inducing story.

Thanks to Tracey for every time she laughed when I told her my brain was rotting from the sweet.

Thanks to Stella for letting me tease her unmercifully with snippets as I wrote it.

A thanks to Jessey for repeatedly telling me all her "babies" deserved all the fluff, all the time.

And a massive thank you to my betas who took time out of their lives to read Grey and Shug's story for me.

ABOUT THE AUTHOR

Siobhan Smile is an author of happily ever afters with a twist. They feature characters of all sizes, shapes, sexualities, gender identities, and races. Reading a Siobhan Smile book lets you escape for a few hours whether that is to an alien world or a contemporary setting, you'll find something outside the norm. Writing books for Siobhan is more than simply telling a story, it's a way for everyone to see themselves get a HEA.

Author Pronouns: Nonbinary - They/Them

ALSO BY SIOBHAN SMILE

Little Love

His to Own, Hers to Claim

Shug's Daddy